NERDELICIOUS

MARY FRAME

Cover design by Najla Qamber Designs
https://www.najlaqamberdesigns.com
Editing by Elizabeth Nover at Razor Sharp Editing
www.razorsharpediting.com

This book is dedicated to my wonderful friend Grace Taylor.
Thank you for your eternal kindness and friendship.
Thank you for sharing all my fandoms! You're literally the only person that understands me most of the time. ;)
But mostly, thank you for being your awesome self. <3

Chapter One

"I WAS BORN TO BE A NINJA."
—Overheard at Comic-Con

I squint in the low light, the hazy outline of the man in front of me coming into focus.

This is it. I'm going to kiss someone other than Jack.

And his name is Dave.

Dan.

Dwayne? I can't remember.

He's good looking. I think. I can't tell anymore. Maybe it's because I chugged that last drink, but he vaguely resembles Tom Holland, if Tom Holland were thicker, softer, and looked nothing like . . . Tom Holland.

We face each other in the darkened strip of space between a fence and the side of a house. Thirty feet away, music thumps and laughter echoes from the backyard, the soundtrack to this poorly constructed seduction. The only illumination comes from a solitary window behind me, casting a yellow square at my feet.

I stare at Dave/Dan/Dwayne as he leans closer, random thoughts pinging back and forth in my mind like a drunk pinball machine.

Do cows dream?

Remember to breathe. This is happening.

His lips are warm.

This is nice. Isn't it?

If they do dream, do they do it all standing up?

Jack was a decent kisser. I think.

Maybe this isn't so nice. He smells a little weird, like beer and cologne and sweat, but I can't really pass judgment. I've been drinking and running around and probably smell a little whacked myself.

His mouth opens and it's . . . *oh, no.*

This is not good. Too much saliva. It's like a wet snake sliding between my lips. His tongue jackknifes into my mouth, and I can't take it anymore.

I yank away. "Hold up there, Casanova." I wipe my mouth with the back of my hand. *Ick.*

He reaches for me with sweaty man-paws, grabbing me by the waist and pulling me against him. "Don't be shy. I'm hurting so bad for you."

He's hard. I know it's supposed to be sexy, his arousal pressed against me and all that, but it's not. It's just weird. Not right. Off. Bad. Peculiar. Discombobulating. Catawampus. Pick an adjective.

My arms are folded between our bodies and I use them to press away, but his grip tightens.

"I'm not shy." You can call me a lot of things, introvert, weirdo, geek, a total fandom-obsessed nerd, but I'm definitely not shy. What I am is pissed off because he still won't let me go. "I don't like being stabbed in the face hole like you have a problem with mouths and you want to murder them with your tongue."

His whole body goes rigid. Hmmm. This may have been a bad choice for my first make-out session post-Jack.

"You're going to criticize *me*?" He pulls away. The better to spew his insults in my face. "At least I'm not a girl named Fred."

"I'm not a girl, I'm twenty-two and a woman, fuck you very much. I just wanted to make out with someone and now you're ruining it with puerile insults."

He stills for a few long seconds, a wall of tension, and then his shoulders relax. An arm slides around my waist. "I'm sorry, baby, I just want to please you." He leans closer, kissing my ear. His mouth is . . . *moist.*

What? Baby? This guy is giving me whiplash but I'm almost too buzzed to care.

Maybe I should let Slobber Man kiss and grope and have his way with me, just to get it over with. I mean, he sucks, but I'll be moving on from Jack. Which is what I wanted, right? Isn't that why I came here?

Slobber Man. More the moniker of a villain than a superhero. His power is drowning people in spit.

I snort a laugh while his hands move up my waist, going for the goods with all the finesse of an off-balance T. rex.

He claws at my breast, and all thoughts of giving in and just letting it happen flee. Nope. Can't do this. I shove him away, taking two giant steps back and coming up against the side of the house.

He lunges forward faster than I thought possible, considering his current state of sobriety. He sets an arm on either side of my head, his hips pushing into mine, trapping me.

I can't believe this is happening. My life has become a hackneyed script, like the writers' room has run out of ideas and decided, *Yes, it would be a great idea to make the Mother of Dragons go abruptly Mad Queen in the last five minutes, sure sure sure.*

He moves in to kiss me and my arms pop up, shoving at his chest. "Back up or my knee will be meeting your ball sack."

I'll have to remember to thank my parents for forcing me into self-defense classes before they allowed me to take the subway.

"You're feisty." He remains unconcerned, crowding me again.

"I'm serious." I raise my voice, jerking my head away from his sodden seduction. "Back. Up." I'm nearly yelling now.

My whole life, I've been prepared to defend myself from muggers on the streets of New York City. But it's here, in small town Texas, where everyone leaves their doors unlocked and children skip around unattended and safe, that I get cornered by a drunken asshat.

As I raise my knee in preparation for an instep stomp, the pinballs in my brain finally come to a stop on one question.

How did it come to this?

. . .

Three hours earlier . . .

"Fred, girl, you get on down here and let that no-good ninny die!" Granny hollers up at me.

I grit my teeth and pull myself farther along the plank, inching toward my goal. "No."

"It's just a dumb bird."

I glance down at her from my precarious position, arms and legs wrapped around an eight-inch beam, clutching it with both arms and legs like it's all that hangs between me and death. And it sort of is. The rope around my waist for "security" is tethered to a hook on the wall and anchored by a fourteen-year-old girl. The only thing between me and certain death is a teenager and a rope.

As someone born and raised in Brooklyn, I never imagined I would find myself rescuing a chicken who'd somehow gotten herself stuck up on a crossbeam inside of a barn. But here we are, hovering over a mishmash of moonshine-making stills and accoutrements.

I scooch closer to the fowl. She stares at me, amber feathers twitching, head jerking, copper eyes flashing.

She's just out of reach. I grit my teeth. "Kylo Hen is not dying on my watch." I don't know if I'm talking to Granny, the fowl, or myself.

"*You* might die on your watch, though," Grace calls up. You wouldn't know it to look at her, pale hair, pixie face, innocent expression, but she's a tenth-level genius with the attitude to match.

"We got eight more in the coop with less attitude," Granny says.

"She's not just a bird to me."

Kylo Hen cocks her head, like she hears and understands me. And maybe she does. I bonded with the terrible creature my first week here. I cried. She pecked at my shoelaces. It was magical.

If anything happens to her, my life will cease to have meaning. Maybe that's a little dramatic, but my whole life has been upended over the last six months and I'm entitled to some theatrics.

Not that your life ever had meaning to begin with, a shrill voice quips in my head, one that sounds exactly like Dolores Umbridge. Evil bitch.

Gripping the board with already shaking thighs, I shoot forward and seize Kylo Hen's feathered body, clutching her close to my chest with one arm. I wobble and tighten my legs to avoid a death plunge.

"Got her." Triumphant, I glance down at Granny and Grace. Surely they are impressed with my amazing chicken-rescuing abilities.

Granny is pacing back and forth, her long grey braids swinging behind her. She's muttering something about supper getting burnt while she's in here dealing with fools.

It's me she's talking about. I'm the fool.

Grace has one hand on the rope, lax and unconcerned, her other hand holding a cell phone up to her face, thumb scrolling over the surface.

Oh, yeah, they're impressed.

I inch back to the ladder, using my free arm for

balance while my legs grip and slide like an inchworm in reverse.

Grace snorts from below. “You look ridiculous.”

I finally reach the ladder, scrambling down in a clumsy, one-handed descent.

Granny stops her pacing when I reach the bottom. “All this for a damn bird that will likely be dinner next week.”

“We can’t eat Kylo Hen.” I hop off the ladder onto the barn’s clean hardwood floor. Since all of Granny’s stills and mash buckets are kept in here, she likes it sanitary. I clutch the chicken to my chest like Granny might attempt to throw her in the frying pan any second.

“Your first problem was naming them.” Granny shoots a look over at Grace, still on her phone. “No more screens.”

Grace shoves the phone in her back pocket and then proceeds to pick at the knot around my waist.

“Is that my only problem today?” I ask.

Grace laughs. “I’m betting you’ll have at least twelve more before sundown.” Her eyes gleam. She loves it when Granny and I squabble, even though it’s not really like we’re fighting or anything, it’s more Granny’s way of showing she loves me. I think.

She’s not actually *my* granny, but she sure does act like I’m part of the family. The part that annoys her.

“Dinner’s about done. You two get cleaned up. Grace, you set the table. Y’all have five minutes.” Granny stalks out of the barn, the door thwacking shut behind her.

The rope goes slack and Grace pulls it away, curling it

around one arm and then hanging it on a hook on the wall.

"She's just worried about you," she says.

"I know. I gotta get Kylo Hen back in the coop. I'll meet you inside."

Grace scampers off to the house and I race across the expansive lawn. It stretches from the back of the house and disappears into tall grass and trees at the back of the property.

If the ranch and surrounding acreage could be compared to a piece of literature, it would be something written by Douglas Adams. Colorful and weird, and yet fitted together with seamless magic.

The chicken coop, for example, is purple, with a lime-green door and a squashed quadrangle of a window that doesn't quite shut. It's likely how Kylo Hen made her great escape. The coop is set back among large trees, nestled into their shade. I open the door and set the chicken down and then make sure everything is latched up tight before scurrying back through the heavy humidity to the house, my mind on the occupants inside.

I don't want Granny to worry about me, or anything else. Have I overstayed my welcome? Probably. I've been here for six months. There's nothing worse than a house guest who can't take a hint.

I enter the house through the back door, thanking the gods of Asgard for air conditioning in the Deep South.

Dishes clang in the kitchen where Granny takes out her ire on the pots and pans. I tiptoe down the hall past the marching row of African fertility sculptures to the dark wood stairs that lead to the second floor.

My little guest room is tucked away on the second floor. It's surprisingly simple, a spot of Jane Austen in the middle of a galactic comedy. The pale blue walls frame a full-size bed with a simple white frame and comforter, an oak dresser, and matching night stands. The rest of the house, on the other hand, is splashed in vibrant colors and spotted with abstract paintings and other esoteric art pieces and figurines.

I grab my Tardis tee, then hustle to the bathroom.

The door is shut. "Grace?" I knock. "Are you almost done?"

"Just a minute."

I lean against the wall and wait for her to finish. The water runs, then shuts off. Then runs again. And off. Then the toilet flushes.

What is she doing in there?

I don't have any siblings of my own, and I thought it might be kind of fun to have a live-in little-sister type. But she hogs the bathroom, doesn't talk about anything important, and when she does open her mouth, it's to ask me incessant questions like, *How long are you staying? Why don't you have a real job if you're a grown-up?* And my favorite, *Aren't you too old for toys?* As if I'd ever be too old for the Baby Yoda Funko POP! figure on my nightstand.

The door opens.

"Finally." I rush to the sink to wash up, but Grace speaks up before I can turn on the water.

"Are you going over to Jude's later?" she asks.

Jude is her older brother, sort of. He lives with Beast, her other brother. Or foster brother, or something. The details are kind of hazy. They don't talk about it much.

The first and only time I asked how they were related, Jude said something about blood being thicker than water, and Granny said she was happy none of them were in her family tree, and then they changed the subject.

"No. Why would I be going over to Jude's?"

"They're having a party."

"They're always having a party." They live walking distance to the local college, making it a prime location for never-ending loops of drinking, carousing, and hooking up. "I'm too old."

Not really true, since I graduated early after taking college credits in high school, but still. Me and parties with a bunch of strangers sound like the seventh circle of Crowley's hell.

"It's the last one," she says with emphasis, eyes wide at my lack of enthusiasm. "Until fall anyway. And by then you'll likely be gone."

"And?"

She crosses her arms over her chest and leans against the doorframe. "So instead of going out like a normal adult, you're going to spend another Friday night locked in your room listening to Halsey sing about how you should be sad?"

"No." I scoff. Yes. Absolutely yes.

She grins, her smile impish. "Come on, Fred. It will be fun. I can go with you."

I laugh. "Beast would murder me with his giant bare hands."

Grace laughs with delight, the devil.

Beast is close to seven feet tall with broad shoulders, stark features, and an eternal five-o'clock shadow. He's a little terrifying. It doesn't help that he doesn't speak. Ever. I don't think I've ever heard him so much as clear his throat. And I'm not sure what his real name is. It can't be Beast. Can it? It's probably a John Wick thing, where they call him *Baba Yaga*, all dark and grim, but he's actually, you know, John.

A cow bell jangles from downstairs.

"Coming!" Grace heads out.

I shove my hands under the water, thinking about the party at Jude's.

Maybe Grace is right. Maybe I should go.

But Jude has his girlfriend, Annabel. And Reese—Granny's biological granddaughter—will probably be there with her boyfriend, Fitz. And they're all nice, but it's like a never-ending happy-couple-in-love fest around them.

The only other one there I know will be Beast. Who I can't have a conversation with, so I'll basically be at a random party by myself. Surrounded by people and yet all alone.

Not exactly enticing since my self-esteem is still recovering from Jack's rejection. How do you move forward when the one who was supposed to love you dismissed you like season two of *The Defenders*?

Downstairs, Grace and Granny are in the kitchen, whispering to each other.

"What are you doing?" I ask.

They leap apart.

"Nothing." Granny grabs a bowl from the counter and bustles into the dining room with it.

Grace grabs a serving spoon and follows her without meeting my eyes.

They're up to something, no doubt.

In the dining room, I slide onto the bench-style seat across from Grace. Granny sits at the head and we reach out, holding hands for prayer.

"Dearly beloved." Granny always starts like we're at a royal wedding.

I close my eyes. Not because I'm devout, but because it's better than staring at the walls, which are painted in three different primary colors bright enough to hurt the eyes. The fourth wall is white, but it's also hung with an abstract mural made up of tiny penises. Penii? Is there a plural? Whatever it is, I don't want to stare at it.

"We are gathered here today to join in our love and appreciation for this fine meal. We thank you for keeping us safe from great heights, devil chickens, and whatever that child is watching on TikTok. Protect our souls from evil hellfire and young boys, especially those of us under twenty. In Jesus's name, amen."

"Amen," Grace and I contribute.

"Will you pass the beans?" Grace asks and I hand her the bowl of green beans.

There's a substantial amount of food in serving dishes set around the heavy mahogany table. Pulled pork, green beans, mashed potatoes, biscuits. One thing about eating in the South is you do a lot of it. Which is not a complaint. I love food almost as much as I love my fandoms.

"Are you going to Jude's party?" Granny asks.

I finish chewing my biscuit and look pointedly at Grace. Then over at Granny. "No."

"You should go," she says, spearing a green bean with her fork. "You could take the Cadillac."

"Really?"

That evil genius. It's not just a regular old Caddy. It's a 1956 Cadillac DeVille convertible. And it's pink. It's atrocious and I love it and she knows it.

When I first came to stay with Granny, I drove her around for her errands. Because of her fainting spells, she didn't want to get behind the wheel, just in case. But she hates people driving her car, especially me. I never had to drive much in New York because of public transportation, and owning a car in the city is a nightmare. I can drive, but I'm a little . . . rusty. As evidenced by the fact that every time I drove her anywhere, Granny would pray for her life. Loudly. Now she's conveniently had zero issues with light-headedness over the past couple of months and no longer requires being chauffeured around town.

Stay strong, Fred. "That's kind of you, Granny, but it's fine. I can hang out here."

I don't miss the glances darting between them.

"Unless I'm not wanted." I try to ignore the sting of rejection. I know they mean well, and I know they're right—I've spent enough time moping around—but it still hurts.

"Of course you're wanted," Granny says. "It's just . . ." She side-eyes Grace before leaning in my direction and stage-whispering, "You know the best way to get over someone is to get under someone else, right?"

A laugh bursts out of me. "Granny!"

Grace is grinning. "Does this mean I can invite boys over?"

Granny points her fork at Grace. "Hell no, young lady, you aren't dating until you're thirty."

"Not fair."

Granny shrugs and takes a sip of her drink. "Fairness is to reality as horses are to pickles."

Grace rolls her eyes with a sigh. "That doesn't make any sense."

"Exactly." Granny turns back to me. "So? Are you going?"

I shrug and push at my food with my fork. "I don't think so. I just don't feel up to it."

"Fine. If you're staying here, you can help with . . . mowing the back lawn."

"Okay. I can help you." I've never actually seen anyone mow the back lawn. It's ginormous and I swear Granny told me it was some kind of buffalo grass that didn't need maintenance. But whatever. It's nice to be needed.

"Fred, no!" She waves a hand at me. "That was supposed to scare you away." She takes a breath and then fixes me with a stare. "Go live your life or I'm calling your momma."

"Ugghhh," I groan. "Fine. I'll go."

Or I'll pretend to go. Various ways to get out of it buzz through my mind like anxious bees.

Anything to avoid a Granny/Mom tag team.

They couldn't be more opposite. Granny owns guns, eats meat, and goes to church every Sunday. My parents are vegans, pacifists, and atheists. And yet Granny and

Mom talk like two best friends at least once a week. And usually about me.

An hour later, we've finished dinner and cleanup. Grace has forced me to pull my long dark hair out of its ever-present braid, conned me into lip gloss and mascara, and maneuvered me behind the wheel of the pink Cadillac.

I'll just go to the diner on Main Street, get a milkshake, and hang out for a bit. Then I'll head back to Granny's. She'll be none the wiser.

There is no way I'm going to this party.

Chapter Two

LOVE HATES that game of words!
It is a crime to fence with life—I tell you,
There comes one moment, once—and God help those
Who pass that moment by!—when Beauty stands
Looking into the soul with grave, sweet eyes
That sicken at pretty words!
–Cyrano de Bergerac

"Welcome to the party of the century!" A nude man, liberally striped with blue body paint, streaks past me.

I jump out of the way of his quivering butt cheeks and land in some bushes next to the sidewalk.

People waiting in front of Jude's house clap and yell their approval of the naked man's pronouncement while I untangle myself from the violent foliage.

The street is lined with cars and the front walk of the house is jam-packed with people laughing, talking, having a grand ol' time, and waiting to get in. Why am I here?

You should turn around and go home. No one wants to see you anyway, Delores Umbridge insists.

I had the best of intentions to avoid the party. I drove the opposite way down Main Street, passed the Frostee Freeze, waved to Ol' Roy—who's eternally chilling outside the H-E-B—and parked at the Finer Diner. Then I sat there and stared through the windows for ten full minutes.

There were—I shit you not—three different couples sitting in booths, sharing milkshakes and fries and gazing into each other's eyes like annoying love zombies.

And that's when my thoughts struck me like physical blows.

First, it's a Friday night and I'm alone, sitting in a car that's not mine, outside a diner I don't want to be at.

Second, Granny is right. I need to move on. And perhaps under someone else.

Third, to actually get under someone else, I need a drink. Something stronger than a milkshake.

I get that making out with some random dude isn't going to fix anything wrong with my life, but maybe it'll be like . . . when they brought Buffy back from the dead and she was all weird and depressed but then she made out with Spike and everything got better. Except for the hellmouth opening and releasing all the uber vampires, and the nineteenth episode of season six where Spike attacked Buffy as an impetus for him to get his soul back and that was *not cool, Joss Whedon*.

But still.

I've seen enough therapists to know I need to challenge my own assumptions and negative self-talk, and I should go to this party. It's good for my mental health in general to be around people.

And the most important thought hits me like Thor's hammer upside the head: I'm sick of myself. My own insecurities. My own thoughts of worthlessness.

I have no idea what I'm going to do with my life, I don't have control over every aspect of my future, but there is something I can control.

Jack doesn't have to be my only. Not anymore. The awareness bursts through me, exploding out of my skin like a glitter bomb that settles in a fine sheen of dust. I need to wipe it away. I need to wipe Jack away. I need new memories.

Which is why I'm here.

If this were New York, I could disappear into a hundred different bars or nightclubs to find a random hookup and then never see them again. But in Blue Falls, options are more than limited.

The house sits back from the street, facing a meticulously groomed lawn that's now being trampled by coeds. It's small and innocuous—at least it is when it isn't stuffed with people and thumping with music. There's a bay window, flower boxes, bright white shutters, and a cheery red door.

During the daylight hours, you wouldn't imagine a Van Wilder type lives there with a bookworm and a giant, but that's the truth. It's like God being a writer named Chuck or Captain America saying, "Hail Hydra!" in *Secret Empire*. You just don't expect it.

I crane my neck to see around the line. Normally,

Beast mans the entry, taking money and letting people in and out, but he's not there and the front door is shut.

The crowd around me is restless and excited, people chatting with each other, hooting and laughing. Someone yells out a plea to open the door and let them in.

Maybe it's full, maxed out, and we're all gonna be sent away. Then I can leave, with the perfect excuse.

A sigh of relief whispers through me.

Taking a slow step back, I run into a wall. A warm wall. I spin around and look up. And up. And up.

Beast.

My heart rate triples. I mean, anyone would panic a little. It's like a biological instinct. I can't control the lizard brain. He's huge. Rugged. His eyes and hair are dark, matching his dark T-shirt and jeans. His lips are relaxed, unsmiling against his scruffy jaw.

"For a big guy, you sure do move like a ninja."

He stares at me for a full beat before his head jerks to one side in the universal motion for "come on." Then he stalks away, toward the house.

Bossy.

Commanding without words. Who knew that was possible? I follow. It's not like I have anything better to do, and waiting in line alone isn't exactly an enticing prospect.

"Are you gonna let us in?" someone whines as we breeze past.

Another calls, "Hurry up, we're gonna miss all the games!"

And finally, a third heckler, "Hey, why's she getting in?" And then louder, "Who are you?"

My response is a reflex born of being raised in a family where incorporating literary references into casual conversation is considered an art form. "I'm nobody! Who are you? Are you nobody, too?"

An awkward pause ensues and then a confused, "What?"

I don't bother looking back. This is why I don't have friends. No one understands my witty references to dead poets.

I trail after Beast up the steps of the narrow porch. He unlocks the door and motions me in ahead of him.

It's not as crowded as I thought it would be. A few stragglers are in line at the bathroom down the hallway, and a couple is making out on the love seat in the living room. A sliding glass door at the back of the house yawns open to the backyard, where the crowd is congregating. I follow Beast through an open doorway on our right, into the kitchen.

He opens the fridge and hands me a can of something, his giant fingers obscuring the lettering.

I take it, reading the label out loud. "Delirium." Surprised, I meet his gaze. "How did you . . ." He can't answer an open-ended question, so I cut myself off. I'm forever regurgitating nonsense around Beast. "I like these. And you happen to have them."

I shouldn't be surprised. Beast is like this. Always watching, always handing people what they need without question. He's always so observant. The first couple weeks after I came to Blue Falls, tissue and cookies would appear on my nightstand, but only on nights that Beast stayed over.

It's unnerving. How much does he see? His dark eyes skitter from mine, and after a tripping heartbeat, he strides past, stirring up a small breeze in his wake and disappearing through the doorway.

"Thank you," I call out, but he's already gone.

I exit to the backyard right as Jude's voice cuts through the air. "Babies! Let the games begin!"

Cheering and clapping meet his pronouncement. From the corner of the expansive patio, Jude lifts an air horn and squeezes. Tonight he's wearing some kind of smoking jacket, per usual. His hair is longish and brown, his posture relaxed. He's in his midtwenties, not much older than the college students he's mingling with, but his aura is larger than life, which gives him the feel of an old soul.

Unlike Jude, Beast is actually a student at Blue Falls University, so I'd wager he's around twenty. But it's hard to tell since he's physically bigger than anyone I've ever met.

Off the edge of the patio, a lawn stretches beyond the light and into the darkness. The yard is encapsulated by a tall fence and a smattering of large bushes and trees.

Clumps of people swarm the grass, running back and forth, competing in some kind of . . . blind-folded, three-legged race. They also have cups on their heads. One couple trips and face-plants into the grass, much to the amusement of the crowd.

There's a tap at my elbow. "Hey, you came."

"Annabel." I give her a quick hug and then we face the competition together, standing side by side.

She links my arm in hers, a red Solo cup in her opposite hand. "I wasn't sure you would drop by." Annabel is a curvy blonde with a wide mouth that's usually got something sarcastic popping out of it.

"I almost didn't," I tell her.

"I don't blame you." She laughs and tugs me toward a table set up near the house. "But since you're here, you have to try one of these appetizers Beast made. I don't even know what they are, but they're awesome."

"Oh." I examine the finger foods on the table—what's left of them. "Looks like a caprese skewer with a balsamic reduction." I pick up one of the sticks and pop it in my mouth. The mozzarella is fresh, as is the basil. I wonder if he got it from Granny's garden. "Did he make the reduction himself?"

She waves a hand. "Probably. I can't keep up with him. They used to rotate who cooked dinner throughout the week, but Beast has basically taken over." She picks up her own skewer. "I don't know why I'm eating this. I'm so full but it's so good. It's like I can't stop myself. So what made you decide to show up?" She throws away the toothpick and holds up a finger. "Wait, let me guess. Granny?"

"Partially," I concede.

Annabel snorts. "I'm surprised she didn't force you here at gunpoint."

"It was close. Where's Reese and Fitz?"

"They're back at the apartment. Making use of their time alone." She grimaces and takes a sip out of her cup. "Let's not discuss my brother and his girlfriend and what they might be doing in our apartment. I've thought about moving in here with Jude, and then Reese could move in with Fitz, but my parents would freak. I caught them making out in the kitchen yesterday when I got home." She shudders. "I eat there. Quick. Change the subject. You want to get in on some game action?" she asks, tipping her cup to her mouth.

I shrug. "Not really. I would rather make out with someone."

It's a bad time to reveal my intentions because the contents of her cup stream out of her mouth, hitting some guy in a football jersey as he's sauntering by.

"Hey!"

She coughs and sputters. "Sorry."

He throws up a hand and stalks off.

Annabel eyes me. "You wanna repeat that, Fred?"

"I've decided that I don't want Jack to be the last man I kissed." The only man. But I can't admit that embarrassment out loud.

Annabel considers me for a second, then nods. "I support that. And I can help. I'll be your wing woman. Come on."

She tows me over to the corner where Jude is surrounded by a small group. Without looking, he reaches back and tugs Annabel closer, turning his face to kiss her once on the mouth before continuing his conversation.

Since my arm is still linked with Annabel's, I get a front row seat to the PDA and the brief but heated glance that passes between them. Jude looks at Annabel like K-pop stans look at Kim Nanjoon.

I avert my eyes and take a few long drinks of my beer.

Jack was never affectionate in public. He said it was vulgar.

"We'll get Jude to help," Annabel tells me. "But first."

Her eyes brighten and then sharpen, scanning the crowd around us. "What are we looking for? Man? Woman? Tall? Short? What's your type?"

My gaze moves over the crowd. The three-legged race is over and people are unwrapping their ropes and blindfolds and putting them in a bucket. "Umm . . . man. Not too big, but not too small. Someone good looking. But not too good looking."

"Okay so someone who looks like a serial killer, got it."

I nudge her with my shoulder. "You know what I mean."

"Not really. If I were you, I'd be going for the hottest guy I could find. I mean, why not? Although you can't have the actual hottest guy, because he's mine."

Jude turns into our conversation and kisses her on the side of the neck. "Why thank you, my dear."

"Hot guys are usually dicks," I say. "Present company excluded. And—" I cut myself off, flushing, not wanting to continue that train of thought. Hot guys don't notice me. They definitely don't want to make out with me, not when they could have someone better, hotter, less likely to bust out obscure movie quotes during intimate moments. I'm not exactly a catch. I'm perhaps better than average looking, but I don't have a real job, and I'm only smart if you need someone for a trivia night.

Self-conscious, I shrug and turn away, examining the crowd. "I need someone like . . ." I tap a finger to my lips.

There are a few shirtless jocks standing in a cluster, but an equally impressive group of ladies surrounds them, all dressed in short shorts and barely-there tanks with silky hair and tanned skin. I'm like a pale ET in comparison.

Next to them, Beast hands one of the jocks a . . . is that a banana? My eyes roam over Beast's impressive figure. Not happening. He's too big and handsome and he doesn't talk and it makes me nervous. Maybe because I can't help filling the silence with pointless chatter, and I have nothing to talk about except fandoms and comics and random factoids passed down by my professor parents.

I move on.

My eyes lock with an unassuming figure in the middle of the crowd of players. His lips quirk when I don't look away. He's not too tall, on the slender side, with dark hair and a slightly rounded face.

Perfect.

I wait until we've broken eye contact and he's distracted, talking to someone on the field beside him.

I point him out to Annabel. "Him."

Her eyes follow my finger and then she frowns, her brows dipping in confusion. "Him? The kinda frumpy guy with the brown hair in the brown T-shirt?"

I nod. He won't have high standards so I'll have a chance. Plus, he's probably a nice guy. He looks nice. He's . . . smiling.

Jude gives Annabel one more kiss and whispers something in her ear that makes a flush spread over her cheeks. Then he steps away, megaphone in hand.

"Babies, prepare yourselves for our next event: the Battle of the Banana Hammocks!" Jude's voice booms through the night.

"Okay." Annabel nods. "We just have to get a big banana between your legs."

"Seriously?"

"Follow my lead." She drags me over to Jude and whispers something in his ear. He nods and winks at me.

Then we're on the move, over to the group where my new potential lover is standing with his teammates.

"Hey y'all! We got one more player for your team this round." She shoves me into the guy and I smash him in the side with an elbow.

"Sorry," I mutter.

Annabel is still pushing at me and I swipe her away.

"It's okay." He smiles. He's got all his teeth. And sure, maybe he could blend in with a tree stump, but I can work with that.

"This is Fred," Annabel says. "She's going first with the bananas." And with that, Annabel flits away.

"I'm Dan," he says.

"Perfect."

"What?"

"Nothing." I clap my hands and glance at my teammates. "So what are we doing?"

There are two others in the group, a tall, thin guy with a faint mustache and his girlfriend, a buxom brunette with a cheery smile and awesome red thick-framed glasses. Dan makes introductions, but I immediately forget both their names.

I'm a little nervous. What if this doesn't work and I make a total fool of myself? It is rather my MO.

Beast appears in front of us, handing me a banana and a twine of rope.

"Thanks, Beast." I smile up at him as I take the items.

Beast eyes Dan and then his gaze swings back to me. I could swear his mouth tightens before he moves on to the next group, but the movement is so infinitesimal I must be imagining it.

"What's up with him?" Dan asks.

"Nothing." I glance from Dan to Beast and then back again.

It's funny. They both have dark hair and brown eyes, but on Beast it's . . . more. Maybe because the width and breadth of him is twice that of Dan. And Beast's features are sharper, more pronounced.

"He's weird," Dan says.

My hackles rise. There's nothing wrong with weird. I'm weird. "He's not weird. He's . . ." I don't know what he is, but I don't like anyone saying anything negative about him. "He's my friend."

Dan laughs. "Sure. Okay, whatever." I open my mouth to make some kind of retort but he cuts me off. "Would you like a drink before the game starts?"

Well. That's sort of thoughtful. "Sure." I smile.

He disappears while the other team members help me tie the rope around my waist, banana hovering above the ground between my feet.

Dan returns, handing me a Solo cup half full of warm beer.

Okay, not exactly what I thought he meant. I pretend to take a drink—I'm not stupid—and smile at him. "Thanks. This is the second time I've been tied up today."

He laughs. "That's encouraging."

Hm. Not sure how to respond to that. He's not even

going to ask for details? Rescuing Kylo Hen is always a good anecdote.

We're silent and I resist the urge to babble. Instead, I ask, "What exactly is this game about?"

"My guess is something to do with hitting the ball with the banana. And I think," he glances over at Jude, "we're about to find out."

Feedback from the megaphone fills the night air, halted by Jude's booming voice. "My good people! The Battle of the Banana Hammocks is upon us."

Whoops and hollers fill the backyard.

"The goal of this event is to use your banana—the edible one only—to push the ball into the bucket on the opposite side."

"All my bananas are edible!" a male voice yells out.

"That's debatable, my friend," Jude replies without missing a beat.

Beast is laying out buckets on their sides about twenty feet away from the row of competitors while Annabel moves down the row, dropping four tennis balls in front of each team.

Jude continues. "It is a relay, so only one banana pusher per team at a time. You must get your ball into the bucket and then run back to give your banana and rope to the next team member to push the next ball, and so on and so forth." He waves one arm with a flourish. "The first team to successfully contain all their balls within the bucket will be declared victorious. If everyone is nearly ready? We will be starting in T minus two minutes." He turns away to talk to someone behind him.

"You all ready to go?" my female teammate asks.

"Make us proud!" Her boyfriend pats me on the back.

Dan lifts his drink in salute. I pretend to drink mine before passing the cup to him. And then it's time.

"All right babies, here we go. Get ready! One, two . . . three!"

An air horn blasts and right along with it a roar of excited cheers goes up from the revelers.

I jerk into motion, swinging my hips in an attempt to get the hanging banana to kick the tennis ball in the direction of the bucket. It's not as easy as I thought it would be. Even though the lawn is trimmed, it's still bumpy and uneven, the ball zigzagging in front of me, and that's when I'm able to hit it. More often than not, the banana sails through the air next to the ball without making contact. Catching glimpses of my competitors swinging their hips with their own flailing bananas isn't helping matters. I spend more time laughing than humping the air like I should be.

"Come on!" Dan yells when I run into the person next to us.

Finally, I get the ball to roll in the bucket and race back. The jock quickly unties me, and his girlfriend ties the banana to him so he can start swinging at the next ball.

"That was hilarious."

Dan is smiling at me again and I start to think this whole thing might work out. It was a good idea to come here. I can get him alone, make out, have a good time, and not think about Jack.

Except I just thought of him.

I won't think of him again after this.

While my teammates kick ass, Beast appears next to me with another unopened can of Delirium and I don't have a chance to tell him thank you because Dan grabs me up in a hug.

We won third place.

With the end of the game, partygoers disperse. Some move into the house. The music kicks up, a temporary reprieve while the next round of games is being prepared for the new upcoming group.

"Want another drink?" Dan asks me.

"Sure." I already have one but . . . I down it quickly and follow Dan back into the house.

Once again, he doesn't ask what I want, but maybe that's because it's too loud to really talk, with the music blasting and all. We sip at some keg beer and glance around the party and strain builds between us like a wall. Which makes me drink even faster. The nerves start to dull as the inebriation sets in and then . . .

"Want to go somewhere we can talk?" he yells in my ear over the music.

I nod.

Then my suitor takes my hand and leads me around the side of the house, and out of view.

He kisses me. It's terrible.

I'm about to introduce my erstwhile suitor to a sprained ankle, but first I give him a chance. "Back. Up."

And then to my great astonishment, before I can ninja kick him into submission, he does back up. Rather rapidly.

"Let me go!" he yells.

Wait, isn't that my line?

It isn't the power of my voice that compels him. He's being forced.

A giant figure looms in the darkness, bigger than The Hulk, holding Slobber Man by the back of the neck like he's a recalcitrant puppy.

"Beast?"

Chapter Three

EVERY WOMAN NEEDS a little madness in her life.
–Cyrano de Bergerac

Beast holds Slobber Man up by the scruff of his neck. The poor puppy is not enjoying the manhandling.

"What are you doing?" Slobber Man's arms pinwheel, but they are about half the length of Beast's reach and he fails to make purchase. "Put me down!"

Beast stalks over to where the fence opens to the front yard. Swinging open the gate, he chucks Slobber Man onto the lawn. He shuts the gate, locking it with unhurried patience.

Slobber man shrieks from the front yard, "I'm never coming back here."

"Good!" I call back.

His voice fills the air, laced with fury. "You aren't worth the effort!"

Even through the haze of my buzz, the zinger hits home.

That's exactly what Jack thought. I wasn't worth his effort either. Apparently, I'm not worth anyone's effort.

Beast stands in front of me, a silent giant. The sounds of the party throb in the humid air between us.

"Thank you."

His face is a blank slate of deep grey in the dim light.

And of course he says nothing, but his gaze is like a spotlight traveling over my face. My nerves jangle. He's probably judging me.

Shame wiggles through me like an insidious snake, hissing louder than his silence.

"I know I shouldn't have come over here alone with some rando, since I barely know him and we were both drinking, but I wanted to feel something other than worthless, which clearly didn't work out for me since he just threw that same phrase right in my face." I should shut up. I need to stop talking but the words bubble up like a geyser ready to blow. "I'm sure you know I'm only here because Granny faked being sick to give me something to focus on other than the fact that my long-time boyfriend dumped me like a box of rocks, because clearly, I am worthless to everyone, including the people who know me the best."

I clamp my lips together to slow the verbal sewage.

He doesn't acknowledge my statements at all. He stands there, staring at me with shadowed eyes while I'm burning with embarrassment.

He can't even nod or something? He might not be

able to talk, but he hears just fine and he knows how to move.

His head tilts. Wait. Did those thoughts come out of my mouth?

He shifts again and part of his face appears in the glow from the window behind me.

"I wanted to kiss someone other than Jack. I know, it's completely lame. But I couldn't stand that the last person I kissed didn't even like me. Now I've kissed two guys, and they both think I'm a piece of garbage. I thought it was bad when Jack was my first and last memory of affection but now it's . . . that guy." I shudder, jerking my thumb toward the fence.

He moves, taking one step toward me. We're only a foot apart, his stride long enough to bring him close enough to touch.

I swallow, gazing up at his dark countenance. Dark both literally and figuratively.

A thought flashes through me like an epiphany. If this were a comic, a light bulb would go on above my head. *What if . . .*

"You know it's only fair." I step closer, shrugging nonchalantly. Or trying to, anyway. I probably look like I'm having a seizure. "Since you chased off my amorous suitor." I reach up, rising on my toes while wrapping one hand around his neck and tugging him down.

He doesn't resist, dropping down into me with ease, like it's the most natural move in the world, us bringing our heads toward each other. That has to count for something.

I close my eyes.

At the last minute his head jerks up and my mouth connects with the underside of his chin.

Maybe I should have kept my eyes open.

He sucks in an audible breath when my lips hit his skin, but other than that, neither of us moves.

So we stand there, him hunched over, while I kiss his jawline. Kiss is a generous word. I'm mashing my lips on him.

Oh no. Embarrassment wraps around me like Mystique changing her skin. And yet I don't move. His face is scruffy, his five-o'clock shadow sharp against the softness of my lips. He smells like fresh soap and a hint of after-shave and it's rather . . . nice. So is being pressed up against him. He's warm and big and there's something inherently comforting about his hulking presence. Like, I know he could throw me over the fence with ease, but he would never.

I should step away. But I don't. And neither does he.

We are a still-life art piece of awkward.

My mouth opens against his skin and the movement startles him to life.

He steps back. His heavy breathing falters. His arms are blocks of tension.

Shit. "I should go." I step to the side, toward the back-yard, and trip over something in the darkness, stumbling forward and he's there, catching me before I fall. His hands grasp my shoulders, righting me quickly before releasing again. He shifts away just as fast, like he's worried if he gets too close, I might throw myself at him again.

Can supreme mortification actually kill you?

In a haze of humiliation, I make it back through the backyard and then into the house without further incident.

"How did it go?" Annabel is like a meerkat, popping up in front of me before I can make it to the kitchen, her brown eyes wide and expectant.

"I need another drink."

She smirks. "That good, huh?"

"I'm an idiot."

She chuckles. "Come on, idiot, let's play charades. I'll get you a drink." She leans in a little and sniffs me. "And maybe some water, too."

I consider arguing, but I'm in no condition to drive. I follow Annabel to the living room and sit next to her on a rose-patterned love seat. A spring digs into my butt cheek, but whatever. A bruise on my ass is the least of my problems. Around me, a group of drunk and happy people play charades. I sit in silence, watching, wondering where I went wrong in my life.

How can I ever face Beast again?

I'm not sure how much time passes, but I'm tired and bed sounds more enticing than binge-watching *Stranger Things*.

"I need to get going," I tell no one in particular. I push to my feet and head for the door.

Before I make it halfway there, a looming presence materializes in the kitchen doorway.

I startle to a halt.

Jude calls from behind me, "Beast will see you home, Fred."

"I can make it myself."

Jude shrugs. "He's intending to stay the night at Granny's anyway."

I could fight it, I guess, but I don't have the energy. Best to get it over with. Can't avoid Beast forever. Can't even avoid him for one night.

He opens his hand and I drop the keys into his giant palm.

Somehow, I manage to keep all my inane words to myself while we walk the dark and quiet block to Granny's car.

He opens my door, which is awfully chivalrous, but I don't say thank you. Can't risk it. Once I open the hatch on my mouth, I might not be able to close it again.

He adjusts the driver's seat back as far as it will go, then takes his time with the mirrors and is he trying to kill me? Finally, he starts the car. Then he drives with both hands on the wheel, at ten and two, eyes forward.

I lean against the window but tilt my head in an attempt to observe him without giving away that I'm staring.

The light of the dashboard gilds his rigid profile. The seat is pushed back as far as it can go, and still he fills up the space, not just with his breadth but with the force of his silent presence.

Even though we didn't actually kiss, even though what we did—what I did—was horrifyingly embarrassing, there is a part of me that doesn't want to run away, cowering in humiliation, although that might be the smart idea. He's . . . intriguing. I want to observe him, like a scientist examining a new specimen.

My eyes trace his features. Strong nose. Hard jaw. He's solid as a rock everywhere but his lips are soft and full.

What would they would feel like, if I actually kissed him? What he would be like, if I could entertain such thoughts? What would he say if he could?

I startle awake, heart pounding.

I'm not in Granny's car anymore. I'm in bed. It's dark, moonlight glowing through the soft white curtains. I fell asleep. How did I get here?

I'm still fully dressed, lying on top of the comforter, sans shoes but everything else is intact.

I glance over at the clock. It's three in the morning. We left Jude's sometime after midnight, I think. I click on the lamp next to the bed.

There's a glass of water, two aspirin, and a folded piece of paper sitting on the nightstand next to the clock.

I take the pills, chug some water, and then pick up the note.

The edge is ragged, ripped from a spiral-bound notebook. My eyes trace over the words, written in careful block script.

Then there's a pair of us—don't tell!

They'd banish us, you know.

My breath catches on a surprised laugh.

He's written the rest of Emily Dickinson's quatrain. I stare down at the words.

No one ever understands the things I say. Except maybe my parents. Jack especially never got it. He would brush me off or ignore me. Roll his eyes at obscure references and jokes that only I could understand.

But Beast knew. He got it. It's such a stupid little thing, and yet . . .

I'm nobody! Who are you?

Are you nobody, too?

Who are you, Beast?

Chapter Four

"THE HOTTEST GEEK on TV is Liz Lemon. It's not up for debate. She's nerdelicious. Her name is even a type of food."

–Overheard at Comic-Con

It's Sunday, which means three major events: church, Sunday night supper, and mandatory check-in with the 'rents.

"Jack is dating your friend Morgan," Mom says. The words pop out of the phone and into my ear in one big rush, like a comic bubble that reads *POW!*

I sit on the edge of the bed and hold the phone away for two full breaths. Then I force it back to my head. "Oh, that's nice." The words are dry on my tongue.

It's a good thing I took this call upstairs in my room and Grace and Granny are outside somewhere. I would never have heard the end of it. Between the two of them, they would have picked and poked until I unraveled. They still might. I wouldn't put it past Grace to have tapped my phone. The girl is a tech genius and as crafty as Puck.

I wince.

"We saw them at Blossom," Dad cuts in from somewhere in the background. "He's still a putz."

Blossom on Ninth? That's where he used to take me when we first started dating, back in high school. It's one of the best vegan restaurants in the city. He knows my parents have a standing date there every Thursday. Was he trying to run into them? So that they would pass the information on to me?

No way. I'm reading too much into it. He doesn't care. Hasn't called. Probably doesn't even realize I'm not in New York anymore.

"We wanted to tell you before you found out from one of your other friends," Mom says.

Friends? I don't have friends in New York, except Scarlett. All my other "friends" were Jack's friends, and now that I'm two thousand miles away, their loyalty reverts back to him.

Scarlett never liked Jack. She's the reason I've been living in Texas in the first place. The ranch house belongs to Scarlett's parents—Granny's son and daughter-in-law. They're never here because they are major artists. Like the really famous, rich types who do shows all over the world, tell everyone they're BFFs with Banksy, and have assistants and junk.

Scarlett grew up in Blue Falls before moving to New York. She hired me a couple years ago to help her with her food truck, For Goodness Cakes. This past Christmas, right after Jack and I split up, I came with her to visit her family for the holidays and ended up staying to help Granny. Granny had some fainting spells, and everyone was worried about her living here, mostly alone, except for Grace. I had nothing else to do. Though, I probably needed to feel useful more than Granny actually needed help.

"Do you care?" Mom asks after I've been silent for too long.

What were we talking about? Oh, right. Jack. Jack with someone else.

Do I? I try to get a handle on the reaction fluttering through my belly.

I care that the person I thought was going to be my life partner decided that I wasn't worth any effort. I care that I'm on a long train to nowhere, twenty-two years old and still clueless about what I want to do with my life. I thought I was on the fast track when I graduated from college early, but here I am, crashed to a halt.

Is there such a thing as a quarter-life crisis?

But do I care that he's moved on? Not so much. I don't want him back. I wouldn't want him even if he begged and pleaded, as satisfying as that might be in theory.

"We're over. We've been over for months. I have no reason to care."

"Have you met anyone new?"

"I don't need a boyfriend." I stand and walk to the window, pulling back the flimsy curtain. Granny and Grace are standing at one corner of the yard and Granny is showing her how to load a shotgun. "Aren't you supposed to tell me to stand on my own without a man and be strong and all that?"

"Well, yeah. I'm not saying you should jump into something serious, but there are surprising psychological benefits to having a rebound relationship. It will help reaffirm that you don't need to be dependent on Jack for meeting your emotional needs. Not that he ever met those anyway."

"Mom, are you telling me to sleep around?"

"No, of course not. But I'm also not telling you not to."

Yep. Tried that. Mission failure. Don't need to relive the other night all over again.

Despite my best intentions, a memory flashes through my mind. Not Slobber Man. Beast. Specifically, trying to kiss Beast. My whole body goes hot with embarrassment.

But then the poem . . . Maybe he didn't mind too much?

Beast isn't my type. Not at all. He's too big, too silent, too intimidating, too . . . everything. But he's also kind. And protective of the people he loves. Maybe overly protective, but it's actually pretty endearing.

This one time, we were all having milkshakes on the patio at the Frostee Freeze on Main Street and a car backfired. Beast threw himself over Grace. The move was immediate and instinctive. A reflex born of necessity and past experience.

There's a bang from outside as the shotgun jumps in Grace's small hands, her entire tiny body listing backward with the force of her shot. Granny grins big. I cough into the phone to try and cover the sound.

Time for a subject change. "I'm starting my job next week."

"Oh, right. The restaurant, Bodean's?"

"Yep." Okay, so it's not really a restaurant, it's more of a dive bar with a side of food, but that's on the list of things I don't tell my parents. I mean, I'm in the middle of nowhere, which is nice for an escape but not so nice for finding a job. Bodean's was the only option.

"Well, that sounds nice. I know how much you love cooking."

She stops and doesn't say what I know she's thinking: I should be doing something more with my life.

We've already had this conversation. The last time was when I took my third part-time restaurant job to help support Jack while he was getting his master's and starting his career.

I never thought about what I actually wanted to do with my life because I was too busy helping Jack with his.

"I have a plan. I've mapped it out. If I work for eight weeks and save all my wages—not even including tips—I could have enough with my other mediocre savings to live somewhere for about a month in New York. That way, even if I don't have a job by the time I get back, I'll have a little buffer."

"You can stay with us as long as you need to, Fred."

More shotgun blasts ricochet outside, along with some whooping and hollering.

"What's that noise?"

"Uh, it's just my roommates." Outside, Granny is wearing her new bright red overalls, grey hair hanging in two long braids down her back. Grace is laughing with the shotgun pointed toward the ground. They start jumping around and cackling like two weird witches.

"What are they doing?" Mom asks.

"Target practice."

A long silence meets that pronouncement. "With guns?"

"Uh, yes?"

"And they're near the house?"

"They're . . . a moderate distance." If moderate distance includes the surrounding yard and immediate area. "Sound travels here. All wide-open spaces, you know."

She sighs heavily and the worry is like its own bullet shot down the phone line. "So eight weeks and you'll be home?"

I drop the curtain and spin back to the bed, flopping backward on the mattress. "Maybe before then. When I have enough money saved, or a job back in the city so as not to be a burden, beholden to all and sundry."

"Have you heard anything from prospective employers?"

"Uh . . ."

"Anything with a 401k?"

"Maybe? There's one place I was thinking about applying. It's a new restaurant chain. It sounds pretty amazing, actually. They have all these fandom themes and the job is—"

"Another food service job? You're too smart to waste yourself at some restaurant. And I know you love the whole comic thing, but can that actually translate into a lifelong career?"

I grit my teeth. She didn't even let me finish. I know she means well, but my parents have worked the same jobs their whole lives, and they have no idea how hard it is to get a job now even with a college degree. Not to mention finding gainful employment that's not going to suck out my soul like a daily dose of dementor.

"It'll be fine, Mom. I'll find something good. I know it."

And then I'll breeze back into town with a new, great job and make Jack and everyone else eat their hearts out. Like when Harley Quinn beats the crap out of the Joker before leaving him in Arkham. But, you know, without all the bleeding.

"Tell Granny to call me this week. I found a great recipe she will love."

She won't love it, it will be vegan and awful and Granny will end up adding bacon to it, but for some reason they love exchanging these things.

"I will. Love you guys."

"Love you, too, Fred baby. We miss you." The twist in her voice sends a corresponding wrench through my gut. As much as they drive me crazy, I miss my parents. This is the longest I've ever spent away from home.

We hang up and I toss the phone on the bed and blow out a breath. I should probably make sure no one shoots their eye out.

I'm halfway down the stairs when the front door opens and a giant steps in.

Beast.

I stop. He does the same, looking up at me, big and silent, his face as impassive as stone.

He's holding a casserole dish covered with foil.

"Oh. Hi." I give a fumbling wave, not sure how to act. So of course I say the first thing that pops into my head. "You like Emily Dickinson."

He stares. I stare back, waiting, for what I don't know. It's not like he's suddenly going to sweep across the room and belt out "The Room Where It Happens," like he's Leslie Odom Jr. except in Texas instead of Broadway. Just the idea of Beast in full dance mode tickles the back of my throat with laughter. I attempt to choke it back but a chuckle escapes.

He frowns up at me and then stalks away.

Smooth, Fred. Why don't you act like even more of a weirdo? That would be brilliant.

I smack myself in the head right as Reese, Fitz, Annabel, and Jude walk through the front door.

"Why are you standing around on the stairs hitting yourself in the face?" Annabel asks.

Where's an invisibility cloak when you need one?

Chapter Five

THERE WAS the allegory of my whole life:

I, in the shadow, at the ladder's foot,
While others lightly mount to love and fame!
–Cyrano de Bergerac

"Dearly beloved, thank you for bringing us all together for this fine meal." Granny pauses for a moment, clearing her throat before adding, "of which I did most of the preparing."

Grace, sitting to my left, squeezes my hand while I press my lips shut in an effort to suppress a bubble of laughter threatening to break free.

"Except for Beast who prepared a wonderful . . . what was it? Potato rosaries?"

"Potato rissole," Jude says, somehow completely straight faced.

"Right, right. Rissole. Some fancy French food," she

continues in a grumble. “It’s a good thing you’re handsome,” she tells Beast.

His lips tighten. Granny can even get the marble statue to crack.

“Please bless this family and all our friends, and in your infinite wisdom, if you see fit to compel Elaine Kilgarriff to share her fried chicken recipe with me, it would be most appreciated. In Jesus’s name, amen.”

“Amen.”

There’s a slight pause and then the table erupts into a flurry of activity, hands grabbing for plates and passing the food around.

“What are your plans for summer, young man?” Granny asks Jude. “You can’t get by on your good looks alone, and idle hands are Satan’s misfits, as I always like to say.”

“I reckon I’ll stay busy. No Satan hands here.” He holds up both hands with a grin. “I signed on for some freelance computer work for people around town.”

Grace’s eternal teen slouch straightens. “Can I help?”

“No,” at least three people say at the same time.

Her shoulders slump and she goes back to pushing food around with her fork.

“I need your help around the farm,” Granny tells her. “Fred’s new job will keep her up all hours of the night, so I’ll need someone to feed the chickens in the morning and milk the goats.”

Grace groans.

“Perhaps you could invite some school friends over to help you while away the lazy dog days of summer.” Jude pours her a glass of tea from the pitcher on the table.

Grace shrugs. "People at school were mean. I didn't really make any friends."

"I find that hard to believe considering your sunny personality." Jude winks at Grace.

She rolls her eyes. "I shouldn't be in school anyway. It's not like I'm learning anything new."

"You promised to try," he reminds her. "And you've said on countless occasions that you want friends your own age."

"Whatever." She shovels a big forkful of potatoes into her mouth.

Reese nods at me. "Fred, I heard you made peach pie?"

I love Reese. She's almost as dorky as I am, but less of a fandom nerd and more of a science geek. Plus she's a whole lot smarter. She reminds me of home, too, since Scarlett is her older sister, even though they don't exactly look alike. It's only when I look closely that I can tell they are even related. Reese is tall and slender with dark hair, and Scarlett is shorter and a redhead. But they have the same refined nose and full lips, and some of their mannerisms are nearly identical. "Yep. From the trees out back."

"You are a goddess. Or a devil. Between you and Beast I've gained twenty pounds since Christmas."

I shoot a quick glance in his direction on the other side of Grace, and my stomach twists. He's focused on his plate. He probably thought I was laughing at him earlier. I have to explain. Without sounding like a freak.

Too late, you filthy muggle, Delores Umbridge tells me.

Last night I was drunk and emotional and he got a front-row seat to my stupidity. Then even more foolishness today, and I don't even have the excuse of being drunk. He probably hates my guts, especially since he had to carry them upstairs last night.

"Where are you working this summer?" Annabel asks me.

"Bodean's."

Jude reaches for a biscuit from a bowl in the center of the table and points it at Beast across from him. "Beast here got a summer job at Bodean's as well. He'll be working security."

I glance down the table at Beast again. What are the odds? Actually, probably pretty high, since there are literally less than a handful of eating establishments in the area. And I know he's on the culinary track at school . . . but security? Did he apply for the kitchen job, too?

"I'll be in the kitchen mostly," I say quickly. "But also helping the bar after food service ends. We probably won't even see each other." Our gazes lock.

I don't know if I'm reassuring him or myself. I force my eyes down to my plate, forking a bite of pulled pork into my mouth. I can't tell what he's thinking. Is he angry we'll be working in the same building? Ambivalent?

The table has been silent for too long.

Can they feel the tension?

"We need to go camping this summer, before Fred leaves and while school is still out," Annabel says.

Fitz nods. "Our parents used to take us up to Lake Richardson every year. We know a sweet spot that doesn't get too crowded on the south side of the lake."

"We'll have to go when y'all aren't working." Reese

nods at me. "Isn't Bodean's closed Sundays and Mondays?"

"Yes." I take a sip of sweet tea.

"I've never been camping." Grace tilts her head, her posture perking up again.

"I've never been either," I say.

Her eyes widen. "Really?"

"My parents' idea of camping is renting a cabin in the Poconos and having only one bathroom for a week."

Grace smiles, but the movement doesn't quite reach her eyes. "That sounds fun, too."

Maybe I shouldn't have mentioned it. I don't know what happened to her parents and why she's being raised by Granny. Even though I want to strangle my parents half the time, I'm lucky to have them.

"When do you start work, Fred?" Annabel asks.

"This coming Tuesday."

Grace groans. "This Tuesday? In, like two days? I hate waking up early."

"Then go to bed earlier," Granny tells her. "Work is good for the soul. Like I always say, to make an omelet, you need to break a leg or two."

A beat of silence while everyone at the table glances at each other, and then the room bursts into laughter. Except for Granny.

"What?" Granny squints at us. "It's a sayin', look it up."

After dinner, it's chore time. Every week, Granny press-gangs us into helping out around the farm. As a method of defense, Annabel, Reese, and I have volunteered as the regular dishwashers. In reality, it's an excuse to stay in the kitchen and out of the heat so we can drink moonshine and talk.

I tell them about my conversation with my parents and how I misrepresented my job hunt.

"I've applied for nothing. I don't even know what to do with my life."

Annabel lifts a spoon out of the soapy water, waving it in the air. "I get it. It's hard to decide and it feels like you're supposed to know everything by the time you're eighteen, you know? But sometimes it just takes longer to find your niche."

"You should do something with your degree." Reese hands me a clean plate and I dry it with a dish towel.

"I have a bachelor's degree in psychology. There's literally nothing I can do with that, unless I go for my master's. I might as well have majored in English lit."

"What's wrong with English lit?" Reese frowns.

I shrug. "Nothing, if you're not concerned with gainful employment. It's a good thing I have experience in food service. Not only because food is awesome, but because at least I can do something. But unless I want to go back to school, I have no chance of getting a job that could support myself with my bachelor's degree."

"Something will come up," Reese says.

"I have no real plan. Everyone has a plan. I'm a loser."

"You're not a loser." She hands me a bowl.

I take it and scrub at it with the towel. "Says the genius."

"I'm not a genius."

"Sorry, says the person who's like a bajillion times

smarter than me and knows exactly what she wants to do with her life. I don't know anything. All I know is that I need to prove that I'm not a useless drain on society."

Annabel rolls her eyes. "You're so dramatic. You're only what, twenty-two? You still have time to figure things out."

"I guess. It just feels like everyone else my age has dreams, goals, aspirations . . . I don't know what I want to do other than go to Comic-Con at least fourteen times before I die."

"Fourteen?" Reese's brows lift to her hairline.

"At least."

Annabel laughs. "That's pretty arbitrary. Look, Fred, don't stress. It will all work out. We'll help you search for jobs, right, Reese?"

Reese nods encouragingly.

Well, if Annabel and Reese believe in me, that makes two of us.

"Hey." I tap on the partially closed door before pushing it open. "Where's Granny?"

"Granny went out," Grace says, her fingers not missing a beat at the keyboard, eyes fixated on the computer screen.

"Where did she go?"

A half shrug. "Oh you know. Wouldn't say."

She's been disappearing a lot, but I don't question her anymore. At first, she would say it was "none of my never mind," and then she told me I was "more interfering than a wet noodle." Which didn't make any sense and didn't really sound complimentary either.

"I'm going to take a walk to the tree house. Wanna come?"

"No thanks." More tapping. "Beast is still around. Maybe he'll want to go. Have you seen him?"

I shrug. "Not since dinner."

She frowns. "Maybe he's in the barn then."

"He's staying tonight?"

Grace nods, distracted by something on her computer screen, so I leave her to it.

I need to clear my head anyway. It's easier to do that alone. Normally, when I need alone time, I crawl out my bedroom window and onto the roof above—there's a level spot perfect for stargazing, but the stars aren't out yet. I try to soak them up when I can, since I never see anything like it back in the city. Too much light pollution for stars, let alone a sky full of them.

There is no sign of Beast as I exit the back patio. He's hard to miss—a cursory glance is usually sufficient to locate him.

I take the narrow footpath between some trees and through the tall grass, shrieking and swiping at giant bugs flying around trying to attack my face.

The heat is oppressive and the bugs are plentiful, but still . . . Texas is expansively gorgeous. The sky is a giant dome that stretches on forever, a blue so brilliant it can hardly be real. And I can see for miles. My destination is a grove of trees about a half mile away. No concrete jungle here.

As if to punctuate that thought, a rooster crows nearby. Nope. Definitely not in New York anymore.

But I'll be home soon, within the next two months. It doesn't smell like fresh grass and wild flowers there. It smells more like sewer and hot dogs. It's not quiet, not even at night. It hums with energy and opportunities. It's where my family is. It's where I've spent my whole life. It's a city full of life and possibilities and, you know, jobs and a future.

Sometimes I wish I could stay here forever and just never go back. But what would I do in Blue Falls? I can't live with Granny forever. As beautiful and quiet as it is here, as much as I've loved it, it's not home. I don't quite belong.

As I approach my destination, a weird bleating trills through the air, coming from somewhere inside the grove of trees.

Did Kylo Hen get out again?

I hesitate at the edge of the tree line for a moment and then step faster. What is that? There are other noises now . . . and it's most certainly not a chicken. Growling and other odd sounds.

Maybe it's an animal. Is it injured?

Injured animals can be dangerous. I slow my steps when it's apparent the sounds are coming from around the next bend—near the tree house.

Someone coughs, not like choking but almost like forced coughing. It's not an animal, it's a person.

Leaning against the trunk, I peek around the tree toward the tree house and then jump back.

It's not just any person. It's Beast.

Is he trying to talk? Or make noises? *He can make noises?*

He's sitting in the tire swing that hangs off of the thick branches. It's a big tire. Hefty enough to support even Beast's imposing frame, although he fills the space and then some.

What do I do? I can't just stay here. I have to make my presence known.

Careful and quiet, I tiptoe back up the path a few yards and then turn around, stomping and whistling as loud as I can.

Except the song that breezes between my lips is the creepy one from *Kill Bill*. Which is also from the 1969 British horror film *Twisted Nerve*. Either way, I basically sound like a psychopath and a serial killer.

"Oh, hey. I didn't know you were here." The words jangle with insincerity even in my own ears. "Uh, what's up?"

I am so, so bad at this.

What's up? *What's up*? Have I lost my mind? I should just shut up. Forever.

A flush of red creeps up his neck. A muscle in his hard jaw ticks.

We scrutinize each other across the short distance of crab grass and errant white and purple flowers that are probably weeds. A narrow creek winds through the trees about twenty yards off, the trickle of the water and the buzz of insects the only sounds between us.

He stands suddenly, forcing the tire to sway behind him, and then it swings back and hits him in the ass.

He flinches, using one beefy arm to still the spinning tire. For a long beat, he stares at me, the tips of his ears going red. Then he paces away, disappearing behind another tree.

Well, that was brilliant.

I sigh and walk over to the vacated swing.

Sitting in the center of the black rubber circle, I push myself back and forth with one extended leg.

I guess that cinches it. Yes, I do suck. Yes, Beast hates me. Or at least strenuously dislikes me. And he's within his rights. I hang out on the tire swing for long minutes, pushing myself back and forth, closing my eyes to enjoy the trickling water flowing nearby.

But then a thumping noise invades my meditative thoughts. A pounding *thwap thwap thwap* getting closer and closer. Twigs snap, cracking in the hot air and then Beast comes barreling around a tree at a full run.

I stand up, heart hammering. What could make *Beast* run?

Feathers shimmer behind him, broad and angry red flapping wings.

Oh no.

Chapter Six

"I'M TRYING to become a bigger Star Wars fan."
–Overheard at Comic-Con

"To the tree house!" I yell at Beast—feeling very suddenly like I'm in *Robin Hood: Prince of Thieves* and Sheriff Nottingham's men are attacking—but there's no need for the shouted command because he's already hoofing it toward the ladder and flailing a hand for me to go before him.

Typical Beast. Even though he hates me and would prefer to sacrifice me to the demon chicken, he sends me up first. I don't argue, scrambling up the wooden structure as fast as my hands and feet can take me.

I clamber into the tree house and Beast swoops in behind me, shutting the door behind us in one move. He's forced to hunch in the cramped space, peering through the star-shaped cut-out opening in the door, and I move to the side to look through one of the square windows, squatting down over my toes.

"Oh, it's Cluck Norris."

Beast casts a sharp glance my way.

"The rooster," I explain. "He gets really protective of the hens but I don't see . . . oh. There she is. Yeah. That's totally Kylo Hen. She's always breaking out of the coop. He must have followed her, and now he's—" Cluck Norris flaps his broad wings, herding Kylo Hen toward the base of a nearby tree. "Oh dear. I think it's a mating ritual."

Cluck Norris is bobbing and weaving around Kylo Hen, who's unusually subdued while she waits for him to . . . do whatever it is roosters and chickens do.

Uh-oh, he's mounting her. I avert my eyes.

"This should be over soon." I have no idea what I'm talking about and that point is punctuated when aggravated squawks and flaps sound from below. I peek out the window. Cluck Norris is prancing around again. Dammit, Kylo Hen is probably playing hard to get.

Chicken porn. I yank my gaze away and check out our refuge. The tree house is about ten by ten and made entirely out of a light-colored wood. Faded drawings speckle the far wall, remnants of Reese and Scarlett's childhood. A weak breeze circulates through two open-air windows opposite the door. It's empty, just a bit dusty and dirty from disuse.

Beast straightens into a sitting position in front of the door, fixated on the antics of our chicken friends.

The small space is filled with the heat of the day. It's also crammed with Beast and me and the silence that stretches between us tighter than a rubber band about to snap.

I won't be the one to break it by opening my mouth and sounding like a lunatic.

After a few more minutes of stony silence, watching the chickens flirt, Beast moves, pulling a small notebook from his pocket. Which is actually rather large. He has large pockets. And you know what they say about guys with big pockets . . .

I shut my eyes. *Fred, stop thinking.*

Nothing. They say nothing.

But curiosity eats at me. What's in the notebook? He has a pencil, too. Besides, there's nothing else to look at. Except fornicating chickens.

He opens the spiral-bound book, scribbles something down, and then hands over the whole thing.

My heart rate picks up.

We've never had an actual, legitimate conversation. It's always just me jabbering on in my nonsensical fashion, or him handing me something to drink.

I've never thought to pass him a note, and a flash of guilt sweeps through me. Why haven't I tried to communicate beyond my own big yapping mouth?

But this is exciting. I feel like I'm being handed the Marauder's Map or something.

The handwriting is neat and concise. There are remnants of paper poking through the spiral binding, pages ripped out in the past.

Cluck Norris? it reads.

A grin spreads across my face. "Yeah. I named all the chickens."

He lifts his brows, dark eyes probing and steady. I still can't believe we're actually having a two-way conversation.

"And there's Kylo Hen. She's down there being . . . uh," I tilt my head toward the window, "courted. There's also Hen Solo. Princess Laya." I smirk. "Get it? *Lay*-a?"

He doesn't make any response, so I shrug. "Yeah that one isn't as good. Oh, and Emily Spinach."

He frowns, then sticks out his hand and after a beat, I hand him the book. He writes something and passes it back.

Emily Spinach isn't a Star Wars reference.

"No. It's the name Alice Roosevelt gave her pet snake. She was Teddy Roosevelt's daughter."

He stares at me. His head cocks to one side.

The notebook moves back and forth again.

Why?

"Why did I name one of the chickens after a dead president's daughter's pet snake?" I clarify.

He nods.

"Because it's funny and random and I find it amusing."

Beast, however, doesn't smile. I shift from my crouched position to sit cross-legged on the floor. I no longer have a view of the chicken liaison, but Beast can keep an eye on them. Even sitting, he's tall enough to see out the hole in the door.

"Alice Roosevelt was a total badass," I explain. "In a time when women couldn't even show their ankles without rebuke, she was smoking, jumping off boats, and riding in cars with men. She was banned from the White House after her father's tenure was over by not just one but two subsequent presidents. She's basically my idol. She gave zero fucks."

He watches me with wary eyes like maybe I will flaunt my ankles at any minute. Which is too late since I'm wearing a tank top and cut-off jeans.

I fidget, sitting up to glance out the window and down at the chickens again, anything to escape the heat of his gaze.

Hm. Doesn't look like Cluck Norris is getting anywhere. He's prancing around Kylo Hen and she keeps skittering away.

Beast has his notebook in one hand, his pencil in the other hanging loosely from his fingers.

"It's my parents' fault," I say.

He raises one brow.

"They always talked about random stuff like that at the dinner table. Emily Spinach, Emily Dickinson. Lots of . . . Emilys."

He makes no response. Not even a nod of acknowledgment. I turn my gaze to the corner where someone scratched a formula of some kind. I squint at it. The Pythagorean theorem? Definitely Reese's handiwork.

I wish he would ask me something else. But he doesn't. So of course I have to fill the silence.

"I'm sorry about last night." At least now I have the opportunity to apologize. And if he wants to tell me how terrible I am, he'll have the means. "I shouldn't have tried to . . . do whatever I did to your chin." Heat fills my face. This is terrible, but it needs to be said. "It was wrong and I shouldn't have tried to force you to do something you didn't want to do. You should have thrown me out with Slobber Man. I deserved it." I count the lines in the wooden plank underneath me, unable to witness his nonreaction.

But he's not unresponsive. He's writing something. I hold my breath, waiting. The scratching of the pencil will render my judgment. The scribbling stops and after a few long seconds when he still hasn't handed over the notebook, I risk a glance.

He's holding the paper up, the words facing me. *I can't be forced. Have you seen me?*

I choke on a laugh and meet his dark eyes. There's something in there I haven't seen before. He's always big and dark and difficult to read, but right now there's a spark of humor crinkling the edges.

He writes some more and then turns the notebook back around.

You are not worthless.

I stare at the words in stunned silence.

I didn't say . . . oh, but I did. Last night. After Dan/Dave/Dwayne took off, yelling about how I wasn't worth his effort. I tried to repress those memories, but apparently Beast remembered.

It might not be Shakespeare, or Emily Dickinson, but those simple words wrench something free in my chest that I didn't know existed until this very moment.

So of course I ruin it and talk without filter.

"I wasn't laughing at you earlier," I blurt.

His brows crease. Hmm. A reaction. Not necessarily a good one, but I'll take it.

"When you got to Granny's and I was coming down

the stairs. I wasn't laughing at you. I was thinking something funny, and you just happened to be there. My brain is weird, in case you weren't aware."

I can't meet his eyes. I stare down at a hole in the board near my foot and trace a finger around it and the sound of the pencil scribbling on the paper gives me both anxiety and hope.

The notebook is thrust under my face and I take it, meeting his eyes warily before reading what's on the page.

What were you thinking that was funny?

I bite my lip. I shouldn't tell him, but I've never been a good liar.

"Honestly?" I hand the pad back and look up into his eyes.

He nods.

"I was imagining our lives as a musical. *Hamilton*, specifically. In my head you were sashaying across the floor and . . . it was funny in my head, but probably not actually funny, and I'm going to stop talking."

Dear Lord. Kill me now. If there were mercy in this world, lightning would strike. The apocalypse would arrive to distract us both from my ongoing ineptitude.

I study the window. Through it, the sun is setting, the sky getting dark enough a star glimmers on the horizon. Chickens are still squawking and cavorting below. Who knew they could go on this long?

Eventually, Beast taps me on the leg and I startle at the contact.

He points toward the door. It's silent. I peer out my little window. The chickens are gone.

He lumbers to his feet, hunching over and opening the door to go out first. I follow him down the ladder.

At the bottom, the final rung is set a few feet from the ground. I turn to look before I leap and Beast is there, arm extended.

After a brief hesitation, I take his hand. It engulfs mine, holding me securely as I jump to the ground. Warm. Strong. My breath catches on the descent.

I release him as soon as my feet settle on the ground. “Thanks.”

We pick our way through the leaves and branches and bramble to the path back to the house. The cicadas are buzzing, the sun is gone, and a soft glow on the horizon casts its final residue of illumination.

Once we reach Granny’s, he opens the door for me to precede him into the house.

I stop at the entrance and look up at him. “I’ll see you at work. Maybe.”

He nods.

I take a step but then stop again. “Did you apply for the assistant chef job there?”

He shakes his head.

“Why not? You’re on a culinary path, right?”

He nods and then covers his mouth with his hand and shrugs.

“They wouldn’t let you work in the kitchen because you can’t talk?”

He shakes his head and then pulls out his notebook, writing something inside and tilting the page in my direction.

Didn’t try.

I stare at the words for a few long seconds. "You know, there's an option on most cell phones to have it read text out loud. If you were wanting to have a conversation without having to use a pen and paper, I mean."

His eyes widen.

I shrug. "Might be another way to communicate. If you wanted to. Thanks for . . . I don't know. Good night."

I rush inside and then up the stairs without looking back.

After getting ready for bed, I open my window and hoist myself onto the roof.

And it's here that I can finally breathe, looking up at a blanket of stars so overwhelming and vast, all my worries are miniscule by comparison.

Inevitably, my thoughts return to Beast.

Why can't he talk? I didn't notice any physical scars.

I should be contemplating my future, my plans to save money, my successful return to New York. But instead I'm contemplating dark eyes and a silent man.

Maybe we'll spend more time together at work. Carpooling, at least. A frisson of something skitters through my belly. Part nerves, part anticipation.

All will be well. As long as I keep my mouth under control.

I scowl up at the gorgeous sky above me.

Such an impossibility. Nothing will be well.

Chapter Seven

"SOMEDAY I WANT to meet a girl who's not in a costume."

—Overheard at Comic-Con

Every kitchen I've ever worked in is basically the same. There is a lot of hustle, chopping, cleaning, and it's hotter than Genosha right after Magneto bombed the island. The only difference at Bodean's is the head chef.

Lucas doesn't bark orders and act all high and mighty like most head chefs I've worked for. Not counting Scarlett, of course. And he's probably as old as Granny, or older. He's from "the Deep*er* South" Eliza tells me, which is her explanation for why he talks slow, and sometimes I can hardly understand him, but his fingers are fast and deft and he preps plates faster than Wally West. And the food, well that's been a surprise, too, considering the stickiness of the refurbished barn floor out in the main area.

Ranger sticks his head through the swinging door,

cowboy hat bobbing. "I'm gonna relieve security for a twenty-minute break. You got a plate for the big fella?"

Lucas, in front of the stove, points his spatula at me.

I'm already on the move. "On it. I'll finish cleanup when I get back."

I prep a plate of the specials for Beast—tonight it's shrimp and grits sautéed in butter with a side of corn fritters. I haven't tasted it yet, but it smells divine.

It's not the bar fare I'm used to, even though there are the requisite burgers, fries, and hot wings. Lucas insists on purchasing only local produce and meats and there are surprising options on the menu, including Cajun boil, Hot Browns, and delicately seared catfish with a side of fried green tomatoes.

Leaving the kitchen, I turn a corner at the bar where the same three thirty-something men have been perched every night this week, drinking identical draft beers and arguing about whether the New York Sharks' record would be better with Brent Crawford as a player instead of a coach. I head down a back hallway, sidestepping one of the roadies carrying a speaker to the stage on the other side of the building.

Ranger's office is where most of us take our breaks because there isn't any kind of employee break room.

I knock on the closed door before swinging it open. "Hey." I set the plate on the table in front of the couch where Beast is sitting, elbows on his knees, cell phone in his hands. The couch is worn brown leather. In the back of the room sits a heavy wooden desk, filing cabinets, and an old-ass computer that was the height of technology before I was born.

He's wearing his requisite bouncer gear: dark jeans with a black T-shirt that has a Bodean's logo on the breast. I have my own black blouse with the same logo. But the company shirts must not come in size goliath because it's on the tight side. The sleeves strain under the curve of his biceps, and the fabric hugs his shoulders, outlining the definition underneath.

He normally wears stuff that's a little baggier so while it's impossible to hide his inherent size no matter the outfit, I didn't quite comprehend his actual form until . . . now. And now I can't stop comprehending it, no matter how hard I try. There's no denying it, Beast is hot. But the attraction simmering in my belly, growing every day, is irrelevant because it's not reciprocated. Every time I think about when I tried to kiss Beast and how weird it was and how he reacted, embarrassment sweeps through me and helps quash any lingering temptation.

He signs a thank-you by holding his palm flat to his face, then moving it forward and down. Then he holds up one finger to indicate I should wait.

Every night for the past week I've brought him dinner on his break. Who knew chicken porn could bring people together?

I figured out he knows ASL by talking to Grace, and I've been taking the time to learn some simple signs. I've got the alphabet down, that was the easy part, and then a few common hand signals like *please*, *thank you*, and *more*, amongst others.

He pushes something on his phone. "Thank you," a robotic feminine voice intones.

I clap my hands together, moving around the table to

examine his phone. "While it's hilarious that you're using Siri's voice, maybe we can change it." I sit on the armrest and lean in, resting a hand on his shoulder to help him adjust the settings. "Oh, do the Australian man voice, I love that one."

He shakes his head and types, *I'm less of a Wolverine and more of a Deadpool kind of guy.*

I laugh. "Yeah, it's all the monologuing and cursing that gives you away."

He looks at me, one corner of his mouth twitching up, the smallest sign of amusement. And just like that, the heat of his shoulder under my palm is scalding.

I stand. "I better get back. I'll see you after closing." I leave with a wave, exiting the room with so much haste I probably leave a smoke-shaped Fred behind me.

We've been carpooling to work together. Sometimes in Granny's car, but mostly we use Fitz's truck. The pickup is more comfortable for Beast, and Fitz doesn't need it since he lives in town with Annabel. She has a car and nearly everything is within walking distance.

Back in the kitchen I continue cleanup. It's almost nine, which means it's time to do the most glamorous part of my job: washing the dishes.

At least they've got a nice, deep stainless-steel sink with a sprayer attachment.

Most of my time at Bodean's is spent prepping plates and side dishes, cutting fruits and veggies, and cleaning up while the kitchen is open. Then I move out to the front and help bartend and wait and bus tables. Basically, I do whatever I'm told.

Before I know it, an hour has passed, the dishes are

done, and I'm taking off my hair cap and apron to help at the bar.

"Fred, table twelve." Eliza places the last drink on the tray. Eliza is the bartender slash manager. I've only ever seen her in black. Like Faith on Buffy, she's kinda brassy, kinda emo. She might stake you, might make you laugh depending on her mood.

Skirting the dance floor, I carry the tray to the table in question, a booth near the back, sidestepping cowboys and locals. A loud country song shakes both the rafters and the sticky floor beneath my feet, threatening the safety of the drinks in my hand. No matter that the floor gets mopped every night, within an hour of opening it's splattered with beer and booze, the smell of cleaning product overwhelmed with perfumes, body sprays, and musk from dancing bodies.

Country music isn't normally my thing, but it's kind of growing on me. I might have to visit Skinny Dennis when I get back to New York—one of the only honky-tonks in Brooklyn.

Table twelve is stuffed with a half a dozen women close to my age—late teens to early twenties. Most of them are bleached blondes but a couple have caramel-colored heads and there's one brunette.

I set the drinks out on the table and they ignore me, continuing their conversation. "I love the strong and silent type," the blonde closest to me says. She's wearing a sparkly top and a short black skirt. Her voice is high and sweet, even if her words are on the salacious side.

Her friends laugh.

"You should invite him over when he gets off work, Caroline," the brunette says. "Or to the party."

Caroline picks up her drink and plays with the straw. "I do have the whole place to myself. I wouldn't want to be lonely. Do you think he would protect me?" She bats her lashes, which incites a round of giggles.

I finish with setting the drinks down and load the empties onto my tray. "Anything else I can get you?" I ask loudly.

One woman shakes her head and another waves me off with a flick of a hand.

I make my way back to the bar, glancing toward the front as I pick my way through the throng.

They have to be talking about Beast, and I don't like it. Maybe it's because we're friends. He is actually a really great friend—once you crack the hard exterior. And I cracked that impenetrable surface, oddball ways notwithstanding. It's like he's my little secret. But that's not fair. He's not mine to worry about. And for all I know, he would encourage their attention. Why wouldn't he? He's young. Single. Handsome.

Over at the front door, Beast is turned away from me, checking IDs, his broad shoulders tapering down to a trim waist and hips. He has a nice butt. Almost as good as Captain America's ass. I blink rapidly, forcing my gaze away.

More people are crowding the bar, and time moves at transwarp speed as I serve and mix drinks with Eliza, cashing out tabs and trying to keep up with the horde. Ranger steps in to help out, too. Despite being the owner, he shifts around the building in different areas, giving some of the staff a break when it's needed and pitching in wherever he can.

Small town, small place, which means we all need to be flexible. The volume of customers is surprising, but I guess there are no other liquor establishments in a fifty-mile radius.

Eliza does last call at one a.m. and then the crowd disperses like a flock of locusts leaving nothing but trash, bar glasses, and spilled beer in their wake.

An hour later, we've nearly finished cleaning up for the night. I'm wiping down the bar and Eliza is closing out tabs. There are only a few patrons left.

Feminine laughter echoes through the emptying space.

A few of the ladies from table twelve are at the front door. That Caroline woman is the source of the laughter. She puts her hand on Beast's arm and then squeezes his bicep. Her friends titter.

Eliza comes up beside me, setting down a rack of clean bar glasses. She crosses her arms. "That's been going on all night."

"What?"

She nods at the door. Caroline is still there. She's *still* touching him. A knot tangles in my stomach.

At my silence, Eliza continues, "Your friend really brings in the ladies."

"I guess."

"You guess? Look at him. He probably has a huge—"

"Eliza!" Face heating, I pick up one of the glasses and dry it off before putting it in the cupboard under the bar.

"What?" She flicks a hand at me, all innocence, and then disappears in the back.

I should avert my eyes, but I can't. Caroline is basically a cross between a peppy cheerleader and a girl-next-door debutante. She's the perfect complement to Beast's large, dark countenance.

Caroline points out the door. Like she's giving him directions.

What is she telling him?

Dammit, I can't see his expression.

Just then, he glances back at the bar, and our gazes tangle for a hot second.

"That glass dry yet?" Ranger asks.

I jump. "What?"

"You've been drying that glass for five minutes now. I think it's good."

"Right." I put it in the cabinet under the bar top and grab the next glass.

When I look up again, Caroline is gone.

Beast is hefting chairs up on one of the tables in preparation for mopping the floors. He lifts and stacks with ease, the muscles in his back bunching and twisting under the tight shirt.

So what if he goes out with the blonde? What do I care? I have no claim on him. We're just friends. But my stomach twists with nausea at the thought anyway, independent of rational thinking.

The drive back to the ranch is silent. For once, I keep my trap shut.

A tight coil in my stomach I wasn't even aware of relaxes when he follows me inside and locks the door behind us.

I offer a quick good night and jog up the stairs before

he can make any kind of visible response. His footfalls plod in the direction of the study.

Getting ready for bed, I'm hyperaware of the house's night noises, straining for any sounds of departure, or the door opening, or the truck starting. Basically, anything that might indicate Beast is taking off to meet up with his new love interest. But all remains silent. The coil in my belly relaxes.

This is unacceptable. Beast isn't mine to worry over. I just got out of a long-term, terrible relationship, and I'm moving back to New York in a couple of months.

Besides, they would make a cute couple. Caroline seems like an okay person. I mean, she and her friends weren't the friendliest patrons I've served, but they were talking and having a good time together, no reason to fraternize with the staff.

Resolute, I get into bed and chant a little mantra as I fall asleep.

Let it go. None of my business.

Chapter Eight

MY HEART always timidly hides itself behind my mind.
I set out to bring down stars from the sky, then,
for fear of ridicule,
I stop and pick little flowers of eloquence.
–Cyrano de Bergerac

I scrub at the bar, attempting to focus on my job and not on Caroline chatting up Beast over at the tables near the dance floor.

We're almost empty, only a few stragglers left. Beast was stacking chairs until Caroline came over to talk to him. Talk *at* him.

Whatever. I'm not watching.

The last week has gone by in a blur of late nights at work, chores around the farm, and continuing to poke at my resume. Which means I stare at it blankly, change a word, think about how I'm not qualified for anything and people would be stupid to hire me, and then I change another word and stare at the screen some more. I sent it out to one employer so far. One.

After a few minutes of successful avoidance, my curiosity gets the best of me and I risk a look. She's still there. Standing too close. She hands him a piece of paper and he takes it. His gaze roves over the page and then back to her.

Her smile falters for a flickering second, but then she leans into him, stretching up to say something closer to his ear. Then she takes his hand, the one holding the note, and guides it into his back pocket.

I gasp. She's touching his butt!

"You okay?" Eliza pauses in her counting, flipping through bills.

"Fine." The word is a bark. I scrub the spot in front of me like it's steeped in sticky dirt.

"Uh-huh." Eliza steps closer to me, lowering her voice. "This wouldn't have anything to do with Miss Blonde-and-Ready over there, would it?"

"Nope."

Eliza snorts and resumes her counting.

Work is great. Lucas and Eliza and Ranger are all fun to work with. So is Beast. Except now Caroline is attached to him like a barnacle almost every night. And despite my internal pep talks to let it go like Elsa, for some reason it makes me feel . . . prickly.

It's not like I *like* him.

So why does something wrench in my chest every time I see her flirting with him?

"Hey Fred, what did the bar ever do to you?" Ranger

sticks his head out of the window between the bar and the kitchen.

"What?" Startled, I twist in his direction.

"If that spot were any cleaner, you could see straight through the Earth."

"Oh. Sorry. I was distracted."

Eliza looks pointedly at Beast and then back at me. "We can see that."

Ranger laughs and disappears back into the kitchen.

My face heats. "It's not what you think. We drove together so I can't leave until all of that," I circle a hand, "is done."

"Well, it should be what I think. It's weird if it isn't." She sighs. "If only I was fifteen years younger . . ."

Ranger's head pops out again. "If you were fifteen years younger, maybe you could count that till faster."

"You're more than welcome to take over, Ranger."

He disappears again.

I finish cleaning the bar and head back to the office to grab my stuff, taking my time, going to the bathroom and washing my hands and splashing water on my face to help get rid of the greasy, dirty feeling. Working in food service leaves a film. Not to mention, the longer I take, the more likely she'll be gone when I get out and I won't be forced to watch Beast with his . . . paramour.

But it doesn't matter.

She's still here. Beast's ears are red, the back of his neck flushing as Caroline pulls away from doing something. Hugging him? She walks out the door. But she doesn't do something as pedestrian as *walk*, she sashays like she's on a runway, hips swaying, dress flipping up with each step to expose perfectly tanned and shaped calves.

She casts one last sultry glance under her lashes before exiting.

The ride home is silent, like it always is. But there's a palpable tension in the air. It's probably all in my head. When I tilt my head to eyeball him covertly, he's the same as always. Serious. Staring straight ahead. Focused on the road.

I practically leap from the car when he stops, yelling good night and heading straight up the stairs for bed. I don't want to know if he's still downstairs or if he's left to meet her. As far as I know, he hasn't actually gone anywhere with Caroline, outside of their conversations at the bar, and I really don't want to know.

But after I've washed up and gotten under the cool sheets, I can't sleep.

I grab my phone to check my email. Maybe I'll have a job offer for millions and I can leave Blue Falls next week and never worry about anything again. To my surprise, there is a new email. It's from the job I applied to last week. My heart jumps for a moment as I scroll over the words.

Thank you for your submission. Unfortunately . . .

Ugh. One of those *thanks but no thanks, position has been filled by someone much more qualified and better looking* letters.

I'm more relieved than upset. It was an entry-level human resources job. I don't even know why I applied, except it seemed like something that wouldn't need a specific degree. But even the junior positions are out of my reach.

I toss my phone on the nightstand and flip onto my side in an attempt to get comfortable.

My stomach gurgles. Staying up late all the time has a way of increasing hunger. I made some hummingbird cake for Grace and Granny yesterday since it's a Southern recipe Scarlett has used before at the food truck. I figured they would like it. I wonder if they left me any. It sure does sound good right about now.

Only one way to find out.

The light is on in the kitchen, casting a glow into the entry. Someone else is awake. I wouldn't put it past Grace to be up late hacking into some kind of illegal server or whatever. Doing shady shit stirs up the appetite.

But when I make it to the kitchen, it's not Grace, it's Beast.

He's leaning back against the counter, phone in hand, dressed in a grey cotton tee and darker grey sleep shorts.

"Hey. You want some cake? If there's any left."

If he's surprised to see me, he doesn't show it. He's pretty engrossed in the phone. But he nods.

I grab two plates from the cupboard and open the fridge. Goose bumps race up my arms from the cool air. I should have grabbed my robe. I'm only wearing flimsy shorts and a tank top. But it's too hot for anything else, even with the AC.

"Milk?" I set the cake next to his elbow at the counter.

He nods again.

The glasses are up high in the cabinet and I have to stretch to reach.

I set them down and turn around to grab the milk. My

gaze meets Beast's, and his eyes flick back down to the phone in his hand.

Was he . . . checking me out?

The thought is a little titillating. But he's probably just comparing me to Caroline. The name is a whine in my head. Caaaaroline. I pour us both tall glasses of milk.

I set his drink down next to the cake and lean my hip against the counter beside him as we both dig in.

After a couple of bites, he picks up his phone. "This is good," the robotic voice says.

"Thank you."

We eat for a few minutes. Beast finishes the whole slice in a few bites, and then he chugs down the milk.

I'm only halfway through my own piece when he picks up his phone again. "Can we talk? So to speak."

A zing of anticipation thrums through me. "Ha. Okay. What do you want to talk about?"

I wait for him to type out the words, taking a drink of my milk and watching him over the lip of the glass.

He stops typing and then watches me for a moment, worrying his bottom lip. "I was wondering if you would help me with something."

"Of course."

His brow lifts. "I haven't told you what it is."

I shrug. "So tell me."

His feet shift and this time he doesn't meet my eyes as the robotic voice speaks. "It's about dating."

"Um." *What?*

His fingers move faster. "I'm not asking you out on a date." Now he looks at me.

Ouch. "Well that's a relief." Good ol' dry humor, so

good at masking feelings of inadequacy. I take a giant bite of cake, chewing it up before replying. "So, you need help dating someone else. Someone not me."

He nods.

Caroline. I'm sure of it. But just to clarify. "The blonde from the bar? Caroline?"

He nods again.

"How would I—" I frown as he continues typing. "How could I possibly help you date her?"

"In case you haven't noticed, I can't talk."

I roll my eyes and gesture at his phone. "You're doing fine. Just use that on your date."

And leave me out of it.

He types again and then his gaze lifts to mine, his cheeks a little flushed as he pushes the speak button. "I don't know how to talk to women. Even with the technological assistance. I need help. Practice."

A tug on my heart. It's actually really sweet that he's asking for help. It's probably not the easiest thing to admit. "So you want me to help you practice dating?"

"Or give me advice."

I shrug. "Get her number and send her a text, maybe. Go from there. She's been all over you the past couple of weeks. I'm sure it won't be a problem."

He shakes his head at his phone, his mouth a thin line. "I have her number. I'm sure she will go out with me. But then what if I do or say something wrong? I don't know how to date. I've never been in a relationship."

"Is that what you're looking for from Caroline? A relationship?" I ask. The thought is perturbing. Beast and Caroline . . . together? Caroline coming over to Granny's for dinner, or hanging at Jude's with everyone, perched like a canary on Beast's lap. The jarring images spit and stomp through my head, like someone speaking Klingon in a *Star Wars* movie. It's just not right. But I don't want to examine those feelings too closely.

"I don't know. I haven't thought that far ahead. Does it matter?" his phone intones.

"Well, yeah, if I'm going to help you, I'll need to know these things. Like what's your goal?"

He stares at me for a long second, then his gaze flips down to his phone. His fingers move quickly. His eyes flash back to mine and then he pushes a button. "I thought I would have to convince you more."

"Well you don't. I'll help you with whatever you want." I don't *want* to watch Beast woo Caroline, but at the same time, he's asking for help. He never asks for help, he only provides it to others. How could I say no? I set my plate on the counter and cross my arms over my chest. "Honestly, you're not going to need much help. Just talk to her like you are to me."

He shakes his head slowly. Then his fingers move. "I'm not sure. I get nervous and don't know how to respond."

"I guess that makes sense." I can't imagine dating when you don't talk—or talk only with a phone. It would be difficult. As it stands, he only communicates with family, and me, so pretty limited. Of course, going on dates when you *can* talk is nerve-racking enough on its own.

"Question. Why didn't you ask Jude or one of the others? And you know, I've only had one boyfriend. I'm not, like, a dating guru or anything."

He watches me for a moment, thinking before his fingers move over the screen. "They are into their own lives." He pauses again before typing. "I don't mean that they are self-absorbed."

"I understand." They are happy, in love, focused on their own journeys, as they should be.

"That leaves Granny or Grace, and they are out for obvious reasons. Besides, you are smart. Even Grace, with her tech mind, never thought about communicating with me via a cell phone text-to-speech function." His jaw tenses, like the thought troubles him.

I lean toward him. "It's easier for me to think outside the box since I'm not in it. She's used to communicating with you without words. If that's all she's known, and it works, there's no reason to use any other method. I've seen you guys. It's like a Vulcan mind meld."

Some of the tension leaves his jaw and one corner of his lip quirks up. This time he signs, *True*.

Did he almost smile? Then he goes back to typing.

"There's something about you that's comfortable."

I laugh. "Uh, Beast? I'm the most socially graceless person on the planet. I've embarrassed myself around you too many times to count, I talk too much, and what I say is usually inappropriate or unintentionally rude and insensitive."

His gaze is thoughtful on mine before he types. "You might say the wrong things, but you also apologize and explain yourself. Most people don't do that. Most people can't admit to any kind of fault."

We lock eyes and understanding zings between us like the old *Pong* video game.

He types some more, breaking eye contact. "And you're brutally honest."

Snort. "That's a nice way to say I'm an asshole."

His mouth twitches on one side.

"Uh-oh, don't go smiling at me now."

He presses his lips together and focuses on his phone. "Honesty is a good thing because I know you'll lay it on me straight."

"And you've witnessed enough of my mistakes that it's not as scary. I get it."

I'm a steaming pile of embarrassment. Which is good for making people feel normal, I guess. And probably one of the many reasons Beast wouldn't consider me in a romantic way.

He rubs his chin with one hand, then types more. "There's something else."

"Oh, goody."

He gives me a look that's equal parts amused and irritated. He types again. "She gave me her number. Do I text her now? Do I wait?"

"It's up to you. Personally, I think waiting is like playing games. If you want to text her now, do it. You can make sure she got home okay. That's innocent enough."

He pulls out the paper from his back pocket and sets it down. Elbows on the counter in front of him, he types into the phone, brow furrowed in concentration. My eyes rove from his profile down to his biceps straining at the fabric.

I swallow and resist the desire to step closer.

He holds up the phone to show me the text, not sending it yet.

Did you make it home okay?

I nod. "You might want to mention who you are."

His brow furrows.

"If she doesn't have your number in her phone already, she won't know who's texting, and it's possible you aren't the only one she's given her number to recently."

He frowns at that, but nods and adds to the text so now it reads. *Did you make it home okay? This is Beast.*

"Good," I say.

He presses send.

"Don't get worried if she doesn't text back right away," I tell him. "Some people like to wait so they don't seem—"

His phone dings.

He swipes it off the counter and reads it, eyes brightening. He stands next to me to show me the text, both our backs to the counter, arms brushing.

That's so sweet!!!! Heart eyes emoji. *I am home safe and sound!!! Thank you for checking on me!!*

I clear my throat. "That's good. That's . . . she's definitely interested. Now maybe ask if she wants to go to coffee." And we'll just pretend she didn't completely overuse exclamation points.

He switches over to a notepad app and keeps the phone in my eyeline so I can watch him key in the words. *Coffee? Not dinner or something?*

"Think of it like a test run. Then if things go well you can ask her to dinner. Baby steps. There's less pressure with coffee, and you'll be able to talk more easily. If you're eating, she'll have to bear the brunt of the conversation, which can be uncomfortable for people not used to sitting in silence. And instead of being obligated for a couple hours, you can make it like thirty minutes if you need to bail or it gets too weird."

His brows lift. He types and I watch. *That's smart.*

"And if she super sucks, you can say nice knowing you, byeeeee."

I hope she doesn't suck.

His eyes widen and he immediately backspaces the words.

I laugh. "You mean you hope she does suck. At least a little. Maybe not on the first date, though."

He shakes his head, a ruddy flush tinging his cheeks.

"You just want to make sure she isn't a jerk. Sometimes you don't figure out people are . . . not good until years later."

I don't have room to be picky, Fred. I'm a disaster.

My heart twists at the self-defeating words. He sounds like me. I put a hand on his arm and look up at him. "You are not a disaster."

He blinks down at me and then averts his gaze to the phone and types, *Caroline seems a lot more experienced than me. I'm inexperienced and I can't talk. I don't have much to offer.*

I squeeze his arm. "You have a lot to offer. You are kind and funny and can probably bench press a car. Don't ever let anyone make you feel inadequate. There's nothing wrong with inexperience. We all have to start somewhere."

He studies my face, as if verifying the truth of my words through my eyes. Then he nods slowly.

I'm still holding his arm. I pull my hand back and take a step away. "Ask her if Monday at two at the Finer Diner works. We're both off work. We can get there earlier and set up a couple of booths next to each other. That way I can listen in."

He nods and types. They chat back and forth via text, scheduling the date and time. It's pretty obvious from the excessive exclamation points and emojis that Caroline is ecstatic.

"Well, there you go. Not too bad, huh?"

He switches to the notepad app. *Thank you for helping me.*

"I'm happy to help."

But the words are dry in my mouth. And I'm not happy. If anything, I'm a little queasy. Maybe it's the cake.

Or maybe it's the impossibility of ever having someone who would put this much effort into wooing me.

Chapter Nine

I WOULDN'T DARE SPEAK to her,

I don't have the brains.

The way people speak and write nowadays makes my head hurt.

–Cyrano de Bergerac

Beast's anxiety is a grey cloud circling the air around us.

"Take a deep breath," I tell him. "You're going to pass out if you don't get some oxygen."

He complies, big shoulders moving up and down as he inhales and exhales.

We arrived fifteen minutes early and thankfully, Caroline hasn't shown up yet.

We commandeered a couple of empty booths near the back. I'm taking the one in the corner, where I can sit with my back to the diner and use the mirror overhead to get a view of the action.

To alleviate the burden of ordering using his phone or

sign language, we already ordered coffees and water. The waitress is being tipped substantially to not mention that I came in with him.

"It will all be fine. Be yourself." I pat him on the shoulder, only a possibility since he's sitting in the booth and I'm standing next to him. I check the front window periodically for Caroline to appear.

He picks up his phone from the table in front of him. "That's a terrible idea," it drawls. Grace changed the voice and now instead of a robotic female, it sounds like Morgan Freeman.

"You're yourself with me."

"That's different. I like you."

I know he doesn't mean it in a romantic way, but a zing zips down my spine anyway, followed by an immediate internal admonishment. I'm here to help him date someone else.

Outside, a small blue Honda pulls into the lot. A blonde steps out, adjusting her purse and tugging at her short skirt as she walks to the entrance.

"She's here. I'll be right behind you, okay?"

I pull up the hood on my sweater and sit in the booth directly behind him, our backs facing each other, my eyes on the mirror in the corner.

I fiddle with the plate of food in front of me, an attempt to not appear suspicious despite the hood covering the back of my head. Thankfully the diner has their AC pumping, otherwise I might be sweltering with this disguise.

Caroline immediately spots Beast from the front door and walks over to his booth, sliding into the red vinyl booth seat across from him.

"Hi! I'm so happy to finally spend some time with you outside of your work." Her voice is peppy, upbeat, with a slight Southern twang. Her outfit is more modest than what she wears to Bodean's, the neckline higher, only exposing slight cleavage. Church cleavage, if you will. A row of demure pearls decorates her neck and her hair is in flowing golden waves. She smiles and she has two perfect dimples, one in each cheek. She really is adorable.

Damn her.

"I am happy as well," Morgan Freeman's voice says.

Caroline giggles and her hands cover her mouth. "Well, if that isn't the sweetest thing. You're so smart to figure out how to use your phone like that."

"It was a friend's idea," the phone spits out a few seconds later.

"Oh." Caroline nods and smiles, and then the conversation stalls. "So, um." She picks up the mug. "Thanks for the coffee." She grabs some sugar from the side and stirs it in with her spoon while they sit in silence.

A text lights up my phone.

What do I say?

I type quickly. *Ask her questions about herself. What she likes to do, what she's majoring in at school.*

And he does.

And it's not too bad. It's a little stilted, but they manage to move the conversation along. Caroline grew up in Blue Falls. She likes to scrapbook and knit. She's majoring in early childhood education because she wants to be a preschool teacher. I can't even make this stuff up.

Hell, I want to date her. The more perfect she is, the more my stomach heaves.

"What do you like to do for fun?" she asks him.

"I like cooking. I'm majoring in culinary science."

In the mirror, Caroline's eyes brighten and she leans in, crossing her arms and resting her elbows on the table. The move pumps up her cleavage.

It's so natural, like she's not even aware of it. She is good.

"You like to cook? You should cook me dinner sometime." She trails her fingers over her pearls and watches him from under her eyelashes.

Beast's ears go red.

He rubs the back of his neck and picks up his phone.

What do I say?

Do you want to cook her dinner? If so, just say you'd be happy to.

Fingers flying, he tells her he does.

Caroline beams at him.

And just like that, I've been rendered useless. I'm like the eye holes in Daredevil's mask. He doesn't need me. Envy claws at my insides. Caroline is confident. She knows what she wants and she goes after it. She might be putting out this whole Suzy Homemaker vibe, but it works for her. I can't even make out with someone at a party when we're both boozed up.

I shake my head and try to focus on the conversation playing out behind me. This isn't about me.

"You're so sweet. And that voice. It's so sexy."

He rubs his neck. I know he's not sure how to respond. I text him before he can ask.

Tell her thank you. I hit send and then sigh and type some more. *And if you think anything of hers is sexy, respond in kind.*

He reads my text and a few seconds later, Morgan Freeman speaks. "Thank you. I like your voice, too."

Hmmm. Maybe we're not quite ready for the sexy talk.

But it's still rather endearing. And Caroline seems to agree because she's looking at him like she wants him to be her next meal.

My screen brightens with an incoming text. *Am I screwing this up?*

You're doing great. Relax.

He takes a visible breath and his shoulders lose a half inch of tension.

Her smile deepens, eyes sultry even in the reflection above me. "We can go somewhere else and do less talking. You won't even need your phone." And then she puts her hand on his and bites her lip with perfect seduction.

She must practice the move. When I try stuff like that in the mirror, I look like a piranha.

Life is so unfair.

His giant shoulders are bunched again. He's frozen.

I send him a text, forcing my thumbs to key out the words. *If you want to go, then go. I can get a ride.*

His head twitches to the side, a denial.

Why wouldn't he? She's cute. She's damn near perfect and she's throwing herself at him. She's all but begging for it. My teeth grind. My hand clenches on the butter knife sitting on the table. I *will not* turn around and throw it at her head.

Then he's typing and Morgan Freeman's voice fills the air again. "I can't today. Maybe next time?"

Caroline sticks out her out bottom lip in a pretty pout. "I'll be out of town for the next two weeks. Family trip to Florida. We're leaving day after tomorrow."

He types. "When you get back then?"

She's all dimples. "That sounds great. I should get going. I have a lot of packing to do." She stands and after a brief hesitation when he remains seated, she leans over, kisses him on the cheek, and leaves.

Five minutes later, we're back in Fitz's truck. We waited until she pulled out of the parking lot to leave the diner together.

I expect Beast to want to chat, but apparently, he needs a minute to process because without a word, we're on the move. We're almost to the road that leads to the ranch when he pulls off onto the dirt shoulder and stops under a tree.

He puts the truck in park and rubs his face.

After a few minutes of silence, I have to ask. "What is it? Why didn't you go with her?"

His head lifts and his gaze cuts to mine.

His mouth opens and for a second my heart stops, thinking he's actually going to speak, but then he pulls his phone out of his pocket and slides to the middle of the bench seat.

I scoot in his direction to better read what he's typing.

I've never . . . the words stop.

I stare at his profile. "You've never what? Had sex?"

No. Yes.

He stops again.

"What is it? You've what, never been kissed?" I laugh.

He's not laughing. I glance up at him in the silence and find him watching me, dark eyes wary, brows low.

"Oh."

He looks away.

"No, Beast." I put a hand on his arm but he won't meet my eyes. "I'm sorry. It's not funny, but it's also not a big deal."

That gets his attention. Eyes wide, brows up. He's incredulous.

He types on his phone. *I'm nineteen.*

"So what?" Another thought makes my stomach drop. "Beast. Oh my god. When I attacked you with my mouth, is that why you stopped me?"

He rolls his eyes so hard, his head circles with the effort. *You didn't attack me. But kind of. I was nervous. I don't know what to do. I'm probably bad at it.*

"So." My brain is trying to put all this together. Beast. This giant, hunky man has never kissed anyone? It doesn't compute. "You've never ever even . . ." I trail off since he starts typing.

His thumbs fly over the screen. *I've never so much as held someone's hand. You put two and two together.*

"I get it, I'm just surprised because you're so—"

He continues typing. *It's not like I've had opportunities. Not until we moved here.*

We stare at each other for a second and then he types again and my eyes fly to his fingers—the large digits flowing across the small phone.

Women will look at me but once they figure out I can't speak, they move on. It's too hard, and I'm not worth the effort.

No wonder he was so empathetic about my own feelings of worthlessness. He knows what it's like.

"Beast, you're worth every effort. If women can't see that, it's their loss."

He shakes his head. If I kiss Caroline, I'll be terrible at it and she'll tell everyone and I'll never date again.

"I get being nervous about it. But if she likes you, and it's pretty obvious she does, she won't care. It won't matter." And actually it's kinda hot, him being all huge and handsome and untouched. Does that make me a pervert?

Is that how it was with you and Jack?

"Yes." I shrug. "Sort of. We were both young. So there were a lot of mutual nerves happening. But then we got comfortable and . . . well, it was never that great, actually. But Jack and I are not you and . . . Caroline. Or anyone else. We were not good together. Jack wasn't good in general. With Jack, sex was about him getting off and not much else."

I should have seen the signs.

It seems like Jack was kind of a dick.

I nod. "*Kind of* being an understatement."

He frowns down at his phone, no longer typing. I scan out the window, giving him a little space to collect his thoughts.

He taps my arm and I turn back to him.

He's holding up his phone in my direction.

We could kiss.

Chapter Ten

A KISS IS a message too intimate for the ear,
infinity captured in the bee's brief visit to a flower,
secular communication with an aftertaste of heaven,
the pulse rising from the heart to utter its name on a lover's lip: "Forever."
–Cyrano de Bergerac

"You want to kiss me?" I ask, incredulous.

His eyes are wide and shocked like he didn't mean to type the words.

Fingers flow over the phone screen. *Never mind. Forget I mentioned it.*

"No." I put a hand on his forearm. "I'm glad you did. I'm flattered."

I'm more than flattered. I want to kiss him, too, even though I shouldn't. Shouldn't kiss him and shouldn't want to. I'm not staying here. He considers me a friend and nothing more. Otherwise, why would he ever have asked me to help him with Caroline?

His jaw flexes and oh dear I've done it again.

The only thing that would make this worse is if I keep talking. So of course, that's exactly what I do. "No. I mean, you're right. We could kiss. That way, you can be comfortable when she gets back and wants to," I gesticulate wildly with one hand, "you know, fool around or whatever. I swear, I can do it better than the last time when I sort of made out with your chin." I end on a grimace. Definitely taking sales off the list of things I could do with my life. I can't even sell myself.

I can't tell what he's thinking. He blinks rapidly, looks out the front window. Lets out a huff and then faces me. His gaze darts for a hot second to my mouth before returning to my eyes.

Then he types into the phone. *But would that be like cheating?*

"No. You and Caroline went out for coffee once. You haven't discussed dating exclusively, and it's only a kiss. We won't do anything else. It's practicing. As friends."

Just a kiss.

"Yes."

He types and then his head whips up to watch me read his words. *You're sure you want to kiss me?*

I laugh. "Beast. You're hot. Trust me, it's not going to be a hardship." My face warms with the words, but he should know the truth.

His brow crinkles in this adorably confused way. *Hot?*

I nudge his arm with my shoulder. "Stop fishing for compliments. I know I don't need to explain that further."

But I don't know what I'm doing. And I'm weird.

I laugh. "No, you aren't. I'm the epitome of weird. My best friends are fictional characters. The weirdest person in this truck is me."

I hold my breath and wait for him to answer. I want him to say yes. I want him to say no. What if this is an awful idea?

But then . . . he nods.

A flash of surprise followed by a fluttering of nerves skates through me. "Okay, then." My mouth is dry.

I angle my body to face him. He watches, his head turned in my direction, but he doesn't move. His frame is rigid, shoulders tense.

"Relax. We're not doing anything crazy, just a simple brush of lips. No tongue. Don't be nervous."

I'm trying to convince myself more than him. My hands are clammy and my heart is thumping like it's attempting to exorcise itself from my body.

He turns and now we're facing each other directly.

He watches me with the same blank expression he's had since the moment we met, but now it's different. Now I can almost reach out and touch the thoughts flickering underneath the surface. The twitch in his jaw, covered by the scruff on his face. His features are hard planes, serious and austere, but there's a twinkle in his eyes mirroring my own curiosity and nerves.

I place a hand on his shoulder. There's no way I can reach his mouth without a little help. "Want to meet me halfway here, big guy?"

After a slight hesitation, he tilts down. I stretch up. With an intake of breath, I lean into him and brush my lips against his. It's no more than a whisper of movement.

But I feel like I'm taking advantage of him or something. I lean back to search his face. He's tense. His mouth was relaxed against mine, but his eyes are screwed shut.

I smile and my nerves flutter away. "Beast," I murmur.

His eyes blink open, then search mine.

"We don't have to do this."

He signs, *I want to.*

"Are you sure?"

He nods.

"Okay. Then relax. Breathe slowly through your nose."

He lets out a breath and then nods again.

"Let's try again. And I'm not going to move, okay? We'll just . . . touch for a minute. You all right with that?"

He nods, faster this time. And he takes the lead, leaning down into me and resting his lips against mine. I keep my breathing slow and steady, letting our lips settle in to get comfortable. For someone who is hard everywhere, his lips are soft and full and warm. I keep my hands a gentle pressure on his shoulders, and after a minute his massive form loses an inch of rigidity and he relaxes more.

I take that as my cue to move. Nothing heavy, a simple slide of mouths back and forth, getting the feel of him. He smells like breath mints and aftershave and soap. My hands float up to curve around his neck, brushing against the hair at his nape. It's silky smooth, the strands gliding through my fingers with intoxicating softness.

He shifts closer, his hands coming up to settle on my

shoulders. Fingers gripping, he pulls me against him. Our lips are still stroking together but now my chest grazes his and I almost groan out loud.

I'm getting hot real fast. There is nothing friendly about any of this. And we haven't even used our tongues. *Oh dear.*

I pull back to meet his eyes and get a gander at his reaction.

He's focused on me with a dark intensity, both of us attempting to analyze the other.

He swallows and his Adam's apple bobs. I struggle to pull my brain cells back into working order.

My breathing is faltering as I pull air in through the nose. This is nothing more than friendly pecking. No big deal, right?

"Good, good." I clear my throat and force my voice into a businesslike tone. "Okay, now we're going to do it again but this time with a little more action. Tongue action, I mean." My face heats. I am such a dork.

He nods, leaning forward again eagerly and I stop him with a hand on his chest. We're so close I can make out individual eyelashes and a small freckle near his temple.

"Here's the thing." I work to keep my tone light. "You want to start slow and kick it up a notch at a time. Don't be like Slobber Man."

His lip twitches at that.

"I mean, you gotta read the mood and not get there too quickly. If you're unsure, it's always best to pull back and work your way up to it, slow and steady. Got it?"

His eyes are fixed on me. He nods and wets his lips.

His soft, warm mouth is like a beacon.

We both move this time, mouths meeting in a rush. After a few seconds, I tease the seam of his mouth with my tongue. He opens and I brush inside. We're both tentative at first, tongues playing together in slow movements. His hands slide from my shoulders to curve up, settling at the juncture where my shoulder meets my neck. His thumb stops against the thrumming of my pulse.

I'm already hot and bothered, but that simple movement along with the tantalizing pressure of his tongue rubbing against mine sends heat flooding through me. And I mean flooding. Fires. Biblical proportions. Desire is a storm ready to eat me alive. But desire isn't a strong enough word. To call it something as simple as desire is like labeling Chris Evans sort of handsome.

I pull away, and his fingers trail the rest of the way up, surrounding my face with his giant hands, making me feel tiny and delicate. We stare at each other, breaths colliding. His eyes burn with the same fire that's raging through me.

His hands continue to be tender even as he reels me in, and then his tongue is in my mouth again. My eyes fall shut and the world disappears. All that exists is me and him and our bodies, this moment, his tongue against mine and his hands surrounding my nape.

I want those hands everywhere. Thoughts of what he could do with those fingers ignites a whole new storm of fire. I need to be closer to him. The urge is more than a craving, it's a requirement. I rub my thighs together while pressing my upper body to his, getting only a hint of relief from the contact. A thrumming pulse pounds inside me. *More, more, more.* The desire battering at my insides is like its own entity, a symbiote with the power to make me even more violent than Venom.

What is wrong with me?

I yank backward, scooting to the opposite side of the cab.

Air saws out of me.

Beast is frozen in the middle of the truck, staring at me like I just reached down and picked up Mjolnir.

"Good, good, that's really good." My voice is high. Breathy. Not normal. None of this is normal. I never thought spontaneous combustion was scientifically possible but I'm revising my opinion.

Damn. This is worse than I thought. And by worse, I mean better. He is a fast learner.

"Is it hot in here?" I fiddle with the AC vent, trying to point it at me but I can't even focus on my own hand movements. It's like my hands aren't connected to my brain anymore. No more brain. Brain mush.

His eyes are gleaming. He slides back over to the driver's seat. The tension between us is so thick, it's like a physical wire stretched between us. I could reach out and touch it.

"I think that's good. You'll be fine. Nothing to worry about." My voice comes out weird. Clipped, yet still quavering.

"Can I ask you a question?" Morgan Freeman's voice asks, startling me out of my daze. He's not leaning in to have me watch him type this time. Probably smart. Keep our distance.

"Right, yes. Of course." I roll my hand in a circle. "Shoot."

He types and then looks at me before the words emerge. "Was it okay?"

A hysterical laugh threatens to bubble out of my throat. I swallow it down. "Beast, that was more than okay."

His head cocks at me for a second and then he's typing again. "Does it always get intense like that?"

"Truthfully? No. Not in my limited experience." Never. I was never this insanely turned on with Jack, not even when we first started dating. Granted, I was only sixteen, but still. The boiling devastation that erupted just now is like nothing I ever experienced with Jack, even as we got older and more comfortable with each other. I never had my brain turn itself off and reboot.

"That's good right?"

I nod. "It was good. It was very good." It was too good. "I don't think you'll need any more of my help in that department. The department of *looove*," I crack with a forced chuckle. *Shut up, Fred.* My hands clench in my lap. I need a cold shower.

This was a terrible idea. The best, most terrible idea.

He puts his phone on the seat between us. Then we drive back to Granny's.

He stops in the driveway, but leaves the truck in idle.

"Not staying tonight?" I ask.

He shakes his head.

"Right. Okay."

His hands stay on the steering wheel, knuckles white with the force of his grip.

What do I do? Shake hands? Hug? Kiss him goodbye? That last thought is too appealing. I open the door and slide out. “Bye. Have a good night. Drive safe. See ya later.”

Shut up, Fred!

He nods, his expression inscrutable, and I slam the door, running up to the house. Beast doesn’t pull away until I have the door open. The tires crunch over the gravel and I don’t look back.

Chapter Eleven

"HE'S OLD."

"Like how old?"

"Like, he was alive before *Supernatural* was even on the air."

—Overheard at Comic-Con

"Have you heard anything about any of the jobs you applied for?" Reese tilts back against the headrest, the better to see me in the back seat.

We're in Annabel's car. Grace is sprawled across the seat next to me, her head against the window, mouth open, snoring slightly. Lord knows when she finally went to sleep. She was clicking and tapping at computer keys in the middle of the night. Grace is lucky she didn't have to wake up with the guys. They left at the crack of dawn to reserve our spot. And Beast and I worked last night. He must be exhausted.

I'm surprised he didn't ride with us so he could sleep

in a little longer, but I guess the guys all wanted his help with hefting the camp supplies.

I frown. Kind of rude of them, actually.

It's been a week since our "kissing practice." If I can even call it that. More like "making Fred explode due to sexual frustration practice."

But it doesn't matter. It's not happening again. There has been no kissing, or mention of the kissing, for the last week, only the occasional question on how to respond to a text from Caroline. Which is a good thing. We're friends. Friends don't make out. Friends don't ogle their other friends from across the bar when they're stacking chairs. Friends don't get flustered when their buddy tosses ornery drunks out of the bar while looking all cut and impressive and intimidating and handsome.

Wait, what did Reese just ask me?

"I have an interview next week." I won't mention the handful of immediate rejections.

Annabel hits her turn signal, and we drive up a winding road, leading us further into the mountains and toward our destination. "Who is the interview with?"

I shrug. "It's a temp job. Some marketing firm. I'm not really excited about it, but at least it will give me some experience with phone interviews I can use for the next application."

A job is a job, right? As long as it pays the bills and I'm no longer beholden to my parents or anyone else. Independent woman, hear me roar and all that. But instead of empowerment and liberation rushing through me, it's more a trickle of meh. Disappearing somewhere to hide from the inevitable future would be preferable.

Reese settles against her seat, still half turned in my direction. "If you could do anything you wanted, what would it be? If there was nothing to hold you back. No excuses or limits."

"Well, there is this one position I applied for, but—"

"No buts," Reese points one finger in the air, "no excuses or limits, remember? So what's this job?"

I hesitate, gazing out the window at the landscape growing thicker and greener the further we get up into the mountain. "So there's this company creating a cross country chain of fandom-themed restaurants."

There's a long pause and I hold my breath. But I don't need to worry about it because Annabel and Reese aren't assholes, unlike someone whose name starts with *J* and ends in *ack*. Neither are they my parents, worried about having a daughter who has a weird job and no retirement fund.

"Fandom-themed restaurants?" Reese asks. "Like dining with comic- and movie-themed dishes and paraphernalia?"

"Basically, yes. There are already similar venues all over the world. The job would involve researching markets prior to opening to assist design teams with menu creation, and also observing user experiences in action and reporting back to a marketing team."

"Fred." Annabel glances at me in the rearview mirror, her voice bright and encouraging. "This is like the perfect career for you."

"I probably won't even get an interview. I'm sure it's competitive."

"But you would rock this job. You have the restaurant

experience, you're great with people and knowing what they want, and you know everything about everything when it comes to fandoms. It's totally your jam."

"Maybe it will work out." The trees are a blur of green as we zoom up the narrow road.

Wouldn't that be the perfect thing to shove in Jack's face? How many times did he mock me for my love of "kid crap"? But the truth was he wanted me to be his beck and call girl. To be fair, he did support us both once he started his job. But at what cost?

"No maybes allowed," Reese says. "If this is your dream, you should go after it no matter what it takes."

"Yeah," Annabel adds. "Don't make us badger you like we do Beast. Our harassment allotment is full."

My ears perk up at the mention of my protégé slash former kissing partner. "What are you trying to convince Beast to do?"

Reese glances over at Grace, who's still sleeping, before she responds, her voice lowered. "We've been telling him he should apply to a better culinary school. We've been nagging him for months. But he won't even consider it."

"He won't leave his family," I murmur.

"It's admirable, and it's obvious how much he cares for Grace, and how much she depends on him." Reese shoots a look over at Grace again. "But sidelining your dreams doesn't do anyone any good. I think that's only part of it, though. There's the other minor inconvenience of not being able to speak. He's never outright brought it up, but I know he thinks it will hinder his chances of success."

I nod slowly.

"We still have time to convince him. He's only like, what, eighteen?" Annabel asks.

"Nineteen," Reese and I say at the same time.

He told me his age right before we . . . I shake the images out of my head. One more reason it's a bad idea. He's nineteen, I'm twenty-two. I'm too old for him. Practically a cougar. Okay, that excuse is weak, it's only a few years, but still.

"I don't know." Reese shifts her focus to Annabel. "You saw how he was when Grace took off last year. He was a wreck. He'll never leave Grace, or Jude, or any of us if he can help it. We're his only family."

"Wait. Grace left? Like ran away?"

Reese and Annabel exchange a glance, and then Reese speaks. "She left where they were living in Valdosta and came here to Blue Falls. Jude and Beast followed. But that's a long story. And it's also why she's promised to stay with Granny and go to school."

And here's my opening. "Does it have something to do with what happened when they were kids, like with their parents?"

This time, Annabel answers. "All I know is Jude met both of them at the library in Valdosta. Jude was still a teenager himself, only seventeen or so. Grace was eight and Beast was about thirteen—but tall enough to be mistaken for a man, even then. I don't know what their past was before that, only that they were on their own." She wrinkles her nose. "Jude won't talk about it, even to me, insists it's not his story to tell. They bonded with Jude because of Grace and her hacking skills, and also because they didn't have anyone else."

"What happened to Jude's parents?"

Annabel pauses before answering. "They're alive. But they don't have a relationship."

I nod, not probing further. I've already poked my nose in more than what's polite.

We drive in silence for a while, each of us lost in our thoughts.

My own inner musings are stuck on a giant of a man with a soft heart and a past so dark that he can't even speak. What has he been through? Part of me is incredibly curious and wants all the answers, but the other part of me thinks the knowledge might break my heart. And who am I to hold his secrets?

I'm zoning out so hard, I jerk when the car stops. We've arrived.

"Wake up, Gracie." Annabel puts the car in park and leans back to nudge Grace in the leg.

She rubs her eyes, heavy with sleep, and looks out the window.

We've parked behind Fitz's truck. Water sparkling in the sun through thick green foliage entices me out of the car.

Jude and Fitz are sitting at a wood picnic table in the center of the campsite, playing cards.

Annabel calls out, "Do you ever stop with the games and the betting?"

"The stakes are high, darlin'. If I win this hand, Fitz is cleaning my bathroom for a month."

"Oh. Carry on then." Annabel waves a hand and then

opens the trunk for us to grab our bags.

A couple other tents sit between the trees surrounding the main area of the campsite. I don't see Beast anywhere, though.

"Can we go swimming now? I already have my suit on." Grace is practically dancing in place, all remnants of her nap blown away at the idea of beach and water and sunshine.

"Let's unpack first and see if there's anything else that needs to be set up. We have to find the towels and everything anyway," Reese says before bouncing over to Fitz. She leans into him for a long hug. On the other side of the table, Annabel greets Jude with a kiss. Like they all didn't just see each other last night.

The sky is blue, the birds are chirping, and the air is fresh with the scents of pine and clean sunshine. At this elevation, the heat isn't quite as oppressive. There are a few other campsites in this circle, but the closest one is about fifty feet off and unoccupied. Our campsite is a wide area of packed dirt and grass. There's a firepit and camp table in the center. Next to the table, I pick through a pile of camping gear, bags, coolers, and lanterns, looking for the bag with my tent.

We brought four tents in total. The couples, of course, each have their own and Beast is sharing a tent with Grace. I have my own little one-man pop-up.

That's me. Cursed to wander alone forever like the Phantom Stranger.

"Has anyone seen—" Jumping at a gentle touch on my arm, I flap like I'm being attacked by murder hornets.

Beast is standing next to me, silent as a statue. I put a

hand on my chest. "You gave me a heart attack. How do you move so quietly even in the forest? Never mind. What's up?"

He motions for me to follow him and leads me past the table and around a few looming pine trees to where he's already put up my tent in a spot of shade. The tarp peeks out from underneath, and the netted doorway is folded open. My sleeping bag is already laid out and ready to go.

"Oh, thank you." It's a good spot, far enough from the happy couples that I might not hear any frisky behaviors but close enough that I won't have to worry about getting eaten by a bear.

He nods at me and then lumbers away, leaving me to toss my bag of clothes and toiletries into the little tent. I pull out my smaller beach bag packed with a towel, sunscreen, and a book. Inside the tent, there's a lantern in one corner and an unopened water bottle in a storage flap sewn into the tent wall.

I smile at the little gestures of comfort. He's so good at taking care of everyone in small ways, but if I learned anything from Jack, it's that the small things matter the most. The big gestures are nothing compared to the minutiae of life.

Heading back to the main area, I pass Grace and Beast.

"Do you have to sleep right by the door?" Grace asks from inside the tent. "You're so overprotective. What if I have to pee in the middle of the night? I'll have to climb over you."

Standing outside the door, facing her, he shakes his

head and crosses his arms over his chest.

"Ugh you're annoying." The grumbled words are half-hearted at best. "Will you blow up my flamingo?"

Granny bought her the giant inflatable and gave it to her yesterday.

There's a flurry of activity near the firepit and camp table, where the others are gathering towels and frisbees and transferring food and drinks from a large cooler into a smaller, more transportable ice chest. A high-pitched humming fills the air as Beast uses a battery-operated air pump on Grace's flamingo.

"Do you have sunscreen?" Annabel calls out.

I respond, "I have some."

"I'm so ready to get in the water," Fitz says.

"Feeling hot under the collar from losing at cards? Riddled with nerves?" Jude drawls.

Fitz snorts. "You couldn't make me nervous if you tried, old man."

"Now, now, puppy, you should respect your elders."

Annabel rolls her eyes. "You're like five years older than Fitz."

"A veritable lifetime."

"Let's go!" Grace yells, already heading down the path between the trees that leads to the shimmering water in the distance.

Beast hefts the cooler onto his shoulder, like it's full of air instead of packed to the brim with food and drinks and ice, following behind Grace.

I meander behind the others, listening to the chatter and laughter as we take the short walk to the beach.

The trees abruptly end in a bed of wild grass that

peters out into a sandy stretch of beach.

Grace tosses her towel and bag on the sand and races to the water, lugging her giant flamingo with her.

Beast trails her, his gait twice as long but still having to jog to keep pace. He catches up to her at the shoreline, squeezing sunscreen into his hand. She bounces on her toes in the shallow waves while he attempts to spread the stuff on her back.

In most ways, Grace fits the narrative of a fourteen-year-old, but seeing her here—it's like she's more of a kid. Granted, she's in that strange twilight between childhood and adulthood. But if what Annabel said bears even a hint of truth, she may not have had much of a childhood at all. Most teenagers would probably think it's lame, being at the lake with their family, no friends to gossip or hang out with, but not Grace.

I lay out my towel and shuck my jean shorts, self-conscious in the plain, black, one-piece suit I found at the general store at the last minute.

Jude pushes open an umbrella, shoving it into the sand and twisting it open with competent ease. "I have some activities planned."

"Of course you do," Annabel says.

"Sarcasm does not befit you, my dear."

She rolls her eyes while he pulls off his shirt in that quintessential guy way, tugging up the back before whipping it over his head.

"I'll tell you—" Annabel cuts off midretort. And I don't blame her. Jude is all golden, tan skin and lean muscles.

"Uh, let me put sunscreen on you." She pats the towel

in front of her and he grins and lopes over, settling down so she can rub it on his back.

Reese and Fitz are on the other side of Annabel. Already shirtless and ready for the water, Fitz hands Reese water from the cooler. Reese is wearing a one-piece, too, so I don't feel so lame. Her suit is cuter though, dark green, high neck, speckled with large pink flowers.

There aren't many people around, one family down the beach with small children, and a group of teenagers on the other side. The teens have music playing and the beat of a hip-hop song tinges the air.

Beast returns to where he dropped his towel next to mine. He whips off his shirt and my mouth instantly goes dry. Jude might be a golden god, but Beast is a tank.

I've seen him in his tight, form-hugging work shirts. I've felt those shoulders under my hands. But seeing him in the bright daylight? It's a whole new world. And you can bet your ass I won't dare close my eyes.

I don't think I've ever seen so many muscles in the flesh. His shoulders are broad and defined, tapering down to the ridges of his abdomen, a sculpture of raw masculinity. He's built in flawless proportion, nothing even CGI could improve upon.

My eyes are greedy little monsters, taking him in.

Fred, you're a pervert.

I force my eyes to his face. He's not watching me, thank the gods. His head is tilted, listening to the others discuss some chicken game.

My eyes narrow in on his full lips. Those lips have touched mine.

Look away, Fred. I engross myself in rubbing sunscreen

on my arms and legs, refusing to so much as tilt my head in his direction.

My intentional diversion isn't long lived because suddenly he's standing in front of me, holding a tube of sunscreen.

"You need help?"

He nods.

"Okay." I nod.

There's a lot of head bobbing going on.

I swallow. "Uh, turn around."

He does and I'm presented with the most beautiful back I've ever seen on a man. *Dammit.*

I squeeze the tube too hard and sunscreen squirts all over my hand and wrist, some of it falling to the sand.

Dropping the container down to the towel, I stare at his back, then down at my lotion-splattered limb. "I can't reach your shoulders."

He kneels in front of me on the towel and all that skin and heavy muscle is even closer. It's all too much. The smell of suntan lotion mixed with sunshine and fresh air and Beast's crisp, clean scent. My brain short-circuits until my chest hurts because I've stopped breathing.

Pull your shit together, Fred.

I take a deep breath and start rubbing. *Oh my*. He's warm and smooth under my fingers, and I do my damnedest to avoid lingering too much on the rigid bumps and grooves of his physique.

I spread the lotion all over his shoulders, swiping down to his lower back just above his . . .

Maybe it *is* better than Captain America's ass. My fingers move closer, like they're no longer controlled by me, but by a force much greater. A Space Force. No, an awesome ass force.

Don't touch his butt, Fred.

I jump away before I can do anything I'll regret. "Anyone want sandwiches?"

"Me!" Reese calls.

"I am feeling rather peckish," Jude says.

Beast reaches out and grabs my wrist before I can escape.

I blink down at him, not used to this perspective. "You want a sandwich?"

He shakes his head yes, then no.

"What?"

He points at himself, then me, then the cooler. "You want to help?"

A quick nod.

"Right. Yeah." It is his thing, feeding people.

I walk over to the cooler, heart thumping like a bass drum in my chest. We'll have to stand next to each other. All those muscles and skin will be right next to me. Maybe we'll both reach for the mustard at the same time and our hands will brush.

Fred, it's just sandwiches! Calm your titties!

"Right," I say again. "Let's do it together."

Fitz snorts out a laugh.

Shit. My face is burning and it isn't from the bright ball of yellow fire in the sky.

"I mean, let's make them together."

It's all going to be fine. I just won't talk or look at Beast for the rest of the afternoon. Maybe the rest of my life.

Chapter Twelve

YOU'RE A GENUINELY GOOD MAN. There aren't many of you left.

—Cyrano de Bergerac

"It's time for extra crispy chicken." Jude claps his hands together with a loud snap.

The sharp sound lulls me out of the after-lunch doze I was enjoying, stretched out on my towel in the warmth of the sun.

Annabel wrinkles her nose at him. "We just had sandwiches."

"Not the food, the game."

"I should have known." She flops back on her towel.

"How do we play?" Fitz sits up on his elbows.

"Y'all know how to play chicken, right?"

I tilt my head. "I assume we aren't talking about the model of conflict in game theory?"

Reese laughs. Everyone else: crickets.

I sigh. "You mean the game in the water, two teams, people sitting on each other's shoulders, fighting until someone falls?"

"Exactly right, Fred." Jude points at me. "The fun version. And this particular variation is extra crispy chicken because the players," he pauses for dramatic effect, "are blindfolded."

Annabel groans.

Fitz nudges Reese with his shoulder. "Let's go first."

"Fine. Let's lose fast, though. I want to read." She puts said book facedown on the towel before standing.

But if Fitz is upset about her threat to fail, he doesn't show it. In fact he smirks and winks at us as Jude hands out the blindfolds. I glance over at Beast, who's sitting on my other side. He shrugs and one side of his mouth tilts up.

"You two can fight the winners of this round." Fitz jerks a thumb in our direction.

I refuse to look over at Beast. "Maybe Grace will want to play."

She's still floating about thirty yards down the shore. She came up to eat the sandwich Beast made her, then she went right back to her floating.

Jude and Fitz splash into the water first. Jude hands handkerchiefs to Annabel and Reese as they join in, chest-deep in the shallow waves. The guys have to duck down to help the ladies get on their shoulders.

"This is sort of terrifying. I can't see," Annabel says after she's tied the fabric around her head, clutching at Jude's head, her hands covering his eyes.

Jude holds on to both of her legs with an arm

wrapped over his chest, his other hand prying her fingers from his eyes. "That's the point."

She smacks him on the shoulder. "The point is abject terror?"

"The point is a slight amount of terror and abject fun."

"Abject fun isn't a thing."

"Are we ready yet?" Reese asks.

"Well it is already entertaining," I tell Beast. "But it will be over quick if Reese is set on losing."

Beast shakes his head and points at Reese.

"You don't think she'll fall on purpose?"

An emphatic shake of his head.

"Why not?"

He starts signing a word letter by letter, and I track his fingers' motions. C-O-M-P-E-T-I-T-I-V-E.

"So all this bluster about wanting to read is to lull Annabel into a false sense of complacency?"

A firm nod.

I laugh. "She's smart, too. Dangerous combination."

Drawn by the noise and excitement, Grace paddles her way back to watch the fight.

Jude counts them down and he's barely uttered *one* when Reese pushes Annabel backward, and then without mercy or hesitation shoves her again—pushing her to the side hard enough that she slips off Jude and into the water.

Annabel comes up sputtering. "Reese! I thought we were friends."

Surprised, I share a glance with Beast.

Told you, he signs.

"I want to play." Grace heaves her inflatable on the beach.

Beast is already up, moving in her direction before she has a chance to ask. "Beast, be my partner?"

Annabel returns to her towel to dry off while Grace and Beast set up against Fitz and Reese. Jude stays near the water to referee.

Reese, still on Fitz's shoulders with the bandana now hanging around her neck, flexes her muscles at Beast while Jude helps put the blindfold on Grace.

Beast moves down further into the water to match Fitz's height so there isn't too much disparity in the reach.

Once Grace is up on Beast's shoulders, Jude issues a countdown to commence the fight.

Despite Beast's secure grip, Reese is able to take Grace down by using one simple advantage: Grace is insanely ticklish. Reese secures both of Grace's hands and then all it takes is a few pokes in her ribs, and Grace surrenders, throwing herself into the water.

"No fair, you're bigger than me," Grace complains.

Jude calls out to me, "Fred, you're up. It's you against Reese for the championship."

"Bring it on, bitch!" Reese crows. Beast wasn't kidding about her surprisingly bloodthirsty nature. She is really into it now. I might be concerned if she weren't also laughing and smiling.

"I don't have a partner," I call back.

"Beast can be your base." Jude waves me over.

I was afraid of this.

I try another tactic. "He was on Grace's team."

Jude shrugs. "He can be both. He's like Switzerland. In size and temperament."

I'm about three seconds away from saying something embarrassing like, *I don't want Beast's head between my legs.* But I manage to keep those words on the inside and force myself down to the water, gritting my teeth against breathlessness the whole way.

Grace hands me the blindfold as she passes me on the beach.

Beast crouches a little, submerging himself to his neck, and somehow I manage to jump and squirm and wrap my legs around his neck. He holds me in place by cupping my shins while he stands.

I yelp as he straightens to his full height, hanging on to his head.

One big hand pats my leg.

"I'm good," I say.

I'm not good. His hands are incredibly distracting. Everything about him is a distraction, the heat of his neck, the contrast of his warm hands with the cold water. But I'm not afraid of falling. Even in this precarious position, being near him offers a strange sense of security even though I'm perched on his shoulders with his head between my crotch.

Don't think about that.

I can't not think about it.

Once in a stable position, I wrap the handkerchief around my head.

"Make sure it's on tight. No cheating," Reese says.

"This is the big championship, get ready," Jude says. Then he counts us down.

Without any hesitation, Reese is on me—grabbing at my wrists and yanking me to the side to try and throw me off-balance. She used the same move on Annabel, and I'm somewhat prepared for it. I jerk myself in the opposite direction while she's clutching at me in an attempt to destabilize her.

It works—for a second. I'm still secure on Beast's shoulders but I can't see what's happening with Reese. I assume she wavers, since she's not on the attack. So I go on the offense with the shoving.

Reese leans back, tugging me with her since she's holding my arm, pulling me forward and to the side. But I'm like a barnacle, determined to hang on. At least then when I go, she's coming with me. Losing my center, I start to slide off, still hanging on to one of Reese's hands. Beast grabs me before my head can go under, although the blindfold falls down around my neck. Reese has also collapsed to the side and I laugh and yell at her. "Not so tough now, huh, bitch?"

She throws her head back and laughs, Fitz watching her with an adoring, awestruck gaze.

I smile at Beast but the smile drops when I glance down at our positioning. I'm still hanging on to him, my legs wrapped around his hips, on his side. Like I'm a toddler or something.

I unwrap my legs and kick myself free, one arm grasping his shoulder, but then something in the water—something slimy—brushes against my leg and with a startled yelp, I attempt to climb him like a tree, my arms gripping him around the neck.

"There's something down there." My voice is high and panicked.

Jude lets out a bellow of laughter before calling out, "It's likely a catfish or something."

"A catfish? You mean one of those fish with the mouths big enough to eat my leg?"

Beast's shoulders hitch under my arms.

"Are you laughing?"

He's never laughed. Not that I've witnessed.

And I'll never know if he did, because he pivots and walks us to shore, cutting through the water with ease, despite my hold making us that much wider and adding to the drag.

"I'm not letting you go." And I don't. Not even when we're back on shore, standing in the sand. I'm still wrapped around him, water dripping off both of us.

After a moment, he taps me on the back.

"Sorry." I shudder and release him. "I hate not knowing what's underneath me. Especially when it's slimy." I slide to the ground, the flimsy material of my cheap swimsuit the only thing between our bodies. Despite the breeze chilling my wet skin, a wave of heat rushes through me.

I jerk away, marching over to my towel and wrapping it around my middle, sitting on the sand.

Beast stalks back into the water, deep enough for the water to hit him in the chest. The quicker to be away from me, most likely.

Grace chases after him. "Throw me in!"

He doesn't react at first, not until she attacks him from behind, looping her skinny arms around his neck.

Beast retaliates by picking Grace up and tossing her into deeper water. They do this for long enough that my arms start to ache just from watching, but Beast remains indefatigable.

After a while of lazing around on the beach, Annabel says she "forgot something" in the tent and Jude goes with her.

Totally code for sexy times.

Reese is stretched out on her towel, reading. Fitz naps next to her, lying on his back with his head close to hers, his hand on her thigh like he has to be touching her somewhere, even in sleep.

After a while, Grace returns and Beast swims down the shoreline away from our group. She wraps her towel around her and sits next to me, running her hands through the sand.

"Where's Beast going?" I ask.

"For a swim. He won't go far."

I shade my eyes to pick him out amid the sparkling water. He cuts through the small waves easily. "I can't believe he isn't tired after throwing you around for the past twenty minutes."

"He is a beast." She smirks. "Hey, that was really funny when you freaked out about the plant." She cracks up, nudging me with her elbow.

"Yep. Hilarious."

Beast disappears around a curve in the shoreline. I frown. "He probably shouldn't go too far. What if he cramps?"

"Stop worrying, he's fine. He's a good swimmer. Besides, he'll be back in less than five minutes. He always keeps an eye on me. Like I'll disappear with the slightest puff of wind."

"It's because he loves you."

"I know. I'm lucky. Beast will never leave me."

I lie back on my towel and Grace proceeds to bury my toes in sand.

She isn't wrong. Beast might be overly protective of Grace, and she might squawk and complain about it, but it's obvious she loves him, and his care. And the fact that he is as reliable as the sun rising every morning. He'll never leave her, never pursue any dreams of his own outside of Blue Falls, not while Grace is here. Despite the heat of the sun on my face, I have to hug myself to ward off a sudden chill.

We stay on the beach until the late afternoon and then head back to start on dinner before the sun dips behind the mountains.

It's exactly like I would have pictured a campout in the movies or something—minus the whole serial killer with a hockey mask thing. We roast hot dogs over the fire and make s'mores afterward. Jude tells stories about men with hooks for hands and ghosts living in the woods, but only succeeds in making everyone laugh.

When the fire has nearly died and the moon is high in the sky, the couples file off to their tents, followed shortly by Grace. Beast and I smother the fire and pack away the remnants of food and then say good night.

But once I'm lying in my tent with the lantern off, snuggled into the sleeping bag, I can't sleep.

Everything is comfortable. I have a nice pad under me. There aren't any rocks or twigs digging into my back.

It's nice and cool now that it's dark. It's quiet, except for the chirp of bugs, which should be soothing, but my mind won't shut off.

I'm reliving the day, mostly the moments with Beast. His hands on my legs, how he carried me when I was too freaked out to really appreciate it. His eyes enigmatic in the firelight while Jude told his stories.

Mostly, I think about how none of that matters because I'm not staying in Blue Falls. I'm going home as soon as I find a job.

The small tent is suddenly stifling. Fresh air sounds good. Maybe I can check out the stars. I bet they're even better here than on the roof at Granny's.

I wiggle out of the bag and take the lantern. Outside the tent, the trees block most of the sky, revealing only a hint of the starry night above. I'll have to go down to the beach. I grab my towel from my tent and head to the path, stepping as quietly as possible so I don't disturb the others, increasing my pace once I reach the path.

The moon casts a glow on the beach ahead. Excited, I pick up the pace. The water is a sheet of black, reflecting the moon above. Before exiting the trees, I click off the lantern to appreciate the sky more fully. But movement in my periphery makes me jerk. On the beach, a large form looms dark against the light sand.

That lengthy figure can only be one person. He's lying on his back, looking up at the stars. I glance back at the path behind me. I should go back. I should pretend I don't see him, or maybe head in the opposite direction, around the bend somewhere else. I should not cross the beach toward him, the sand cool on my toes. His head turns in my direction, watching my approach.

I stop beside his towel and stare. He's spread out on the sand like a big buffet of man-meat, dressed only in a thin shirt and sleep shorts. One hand is splayed behind his head, emphasizing the line of his bicep.

"Can I join you?"

Chapter Thirteen

ALL OUR SOULS are written in our eyes.
—Cyrano de Bergerac

Beast nods, the gesture a quick jerk. I might have missed it if I hadn't been staring so hard.

I shake out my towel, setting it down next to his, and then lie down beside him, inhaling a deep breath and gazing up at the stars.

"Wow." The sky is a glittering blanket above us.

It's not exactly cold, but the air has a bite. I pluck at the bottom of my shorts. Then the hem of my tank top, trying to get comfortable.

Beast shifts next to me and then scoots closer, close enough that our heads are nearly touching and the heat of him presses along my left side. He lifts his phone so we can both see the screen, his arm brushing mine with the motion, and types on a blank note page.

Do you miss New York?

I contemplate the random question for a few seconds before answering. "Yeah. My parents. The excitement. There's always something to do, somewhere to go. We've got the best art in the world and Broadway, not to mention the most diverse and innovative food that you can find. There's something for everyone. And there's this energy. It's hard to describe, but the city itself has a pulse —like history has etched its heartbeat into the streets. You could watch an acrobat perform in your subway car one minute and then take a ride on a horse-drawn carriage in the park the next. There really is no other place like it."

Beast watches me with wistful eyes.

It sounds amazing.

"Would you want to go? To New York?"

Maybe. Someday.

I nod and gaze up at the sky with a sigh. "Can't see the stars like this, though."

Do you miss your friends?

"Well, I miss Scarlett. But other than her . . . all my friends were Jack's friends."

Their loss.

"Is it a loss if we never had each other to begin with?"

Our eyes lock for second, his features exposed only by the soft glow of the phone.

Do you miss Jack?

I turn back up to the sky, unable to handle the intimacy of the moment while talking about the five years I spent in Azkaban.

"I miss feeling like I belonged somewhere. But all things considered, I'm glad it's over. He never really understood me. We never would have been happy in the long run. When we first met, in high school, we were into a lot of the same things. Comics, *Magic: The Gathering*, nerdy stuff. As we got older, Jack would tell me it was all a waste of time. He was too old, too mature for the things we used to love. He worked in finance. Did I tell you that?"

He shakes his head.

"He got his master's in financial management. That's what he worked on while I supported him. And once he got a job and started making money, he . . . changed. I took care of everything, bills, dinners, cleaning, and I worked part-time. Yet despite providing so much, everything he did was serious and adult-like and everything I still loved was infantile. Annoying. A hindrance to his wannabe jet-setting lifestyle. I didn't belong in his world."

There's something comforting about sharing these details under the cover of the night sky. Like it's a temple where you can reveal your sins and secrets and all will be forgiven.

He types again, the words coming to life on the screen. *I get it. The not belonging thing.*

"Do you? You have a great family. You go to school. You have goals and dreams. You belong here. I'm basically a homeless wretch."

He nudges me with his elbow before typing again. *You are not a wretch.*

"But I am homeless?" A giggle bubbles out of me.

He shrugs.

"I mean, it's not inaccurate, you're right."

This is the only place I fit in—with Jude and Grace. Both of them are brilliant, though. I can't even speak.

I gasp in shock. "You can't?"

He stares at me, eyes wide. For a split second I think he's going to be pissed but then he slaps a hand over his mouth and turns into me, hiding his face between my arm and the towel, his body shaking.

"You're laughing." I smack his shaking shoulder. "I finally get you to cave and all I had to do was make a terribly insensitive joke." I laugh with him, my voice the only sound filling the night, but his quiet mirth is the best thing I've never heard.

Eventually, he flops onto his back again, and we're motionless together, breathing in the crisp mountain air.

I've wanted to ask him something for a while, though I didn't want to offend him. But now, after that little laughing spell, I bet no one ever talks to Beast about his silence. Grace and Jude are used to it, and everyone else is probably too scared.

"Hey, remember when we got attacked by the rooster?" I ask.

He shrugs, lifting his hands in a gesture of *How could I forget?*

"Yeah, right? Good times. I heard you, before I came through the trees. Were you . . . are you still working on talking?"

He turns his head on the blanket. Our eyes meet. He nods.

"Why can't you speak?" The question is a whisper.

He bites his lip, drawing my eyes to his mouth. But then he's typing again and I have to look away to read the words.

It's . . . his fingers halt. Then start again. *I don't want you to think badly of me.*

"That's basically impossible. I would never think badly of you."

He shrugs.

"You take care of everyone, Beast. You notice when people need something and you provide it, whether it's a cup of coffee or a taste of home or tissues for a broken girl you don't even know."

He watches me as I speak, tracing my features with his warm gaze, like he's searching for truth in the words, before he types again. *If you knew everything about me, you wouldn't look at me the same.*

I turn toward him, lying on my side. "How do I look at you now?" The words are a whisper.

Our eyes lock and then his flicker to my lips.

My heart stutters.

Like I'm normal. Like you care. Like I matter.

"Because you are and I do. You do. I have to admit though, you were kind of intimidating at first. For like the first five months of our acquaintance."

I'm too big.

I smack him on his shoulder. "You're not. You're perfect exactly as you are."

So are you. You were never a broken girl. Only a homeless wretch.

I laugh and he smiles at me, a small one, but it's there, the curve of his cheek glowing under the moonlight. Our faces are only inches apart.

I take a breath, about to speak, but then we're kissing.

I don't know who moves first, but the connection is

instant, his mouth moving over mine, his hands spearing into my hair to lock me in place. I part my lips and his tongue slips inside. It's like we've done this a million times.

It's just as good as before. Better even, because we're lying out in the open air instead of the confines of the truck. I can press the rest of my body against him. I can run my hands up his arms to his shoulders. I can hitch one leg over his waist.

One of his hands glides from my head down to my thigh, then to the side of my hip, grasping me in blunt possession and tugging me closer. Close enough to feel the hard length of him between us. I suck in a breath and desire ricochets through me. He's hard and huge, the size befitting the rest of him. What would he feel like inside? The thought trips through me, adding another layer of arousal.

I edge up and push at his shoulder. He rolls over onto his back, stretched out before me like a sacrifice. A huge, hot sacrifice. I straddle him, centering myself right over the bulge of his arousal. Our clothes are still on, but the thin fabric is no barrier.

We stare at each other for a hot minute, the visual connection nearly tangible, both of us breathing like we've been running miles. My hands fist his shirt. If lust had a color it would be Beast's eyes in the moonlight.

I grind against him and he sucks in a breath, his fingers spasming against my hips. Leaning down, I kiss the breath from his mouth and set up a small rhythm, shifting against him, enjoying the play of soft material between us.

The desire, already an inferno, expands. I lean back to enjoy the view of him underneath me.

He feels so good. Perfect. His hands link with mine and I tug them up, cupping them over my breasts.

I groan, loud in the silent air and he crunches up to cover the noise with his mouth. I'm panting into him, frantic, hips moving against him.

He leans back, and air whooshes out of him in one hot breath. His fingers tremble against my tank top. I show him exactly what I want and he's eager to learn, his hands moving with greater speed at my direction and then his thumbs brushing, oh so carefully, at my nipples through the slinky fabric. I have to keep moving or I'll die. Grinding against him is the only relief and I need it because this craving inside has teeth. And claws digging into me. Adamantium claws.

He collapses back onto the towel, his breathing heavy, his eyes dark and focused on me, his hands moving back to my breasts. He bites his lip, his eyes taking in everything like he doesn't even know where to look. Hands slide under my top, then under my demi bra, the hot skin-to-skin touches nearly tossing me over the edge.

I pant and moan his name and then the orgasm shudders through me, quaking my entire being. The world goes dark as my eyes fall shut and I collapse on top of him.

His arms slide around me, holding tight and then he makes a noise, too, something I haven't heard other than that day in the woods, a kind of murmuring rumble brushing my ear. His fingers grip my hips, moving me against him as he frantically thrusts. His erection spasms against my still sensitive core as he finds his own release.

We stay there, foreheads touching, sharing air.

"That was . . . that was . . ." I can't think. No words. My mind is blank, my body sated and boneless.

His hands rub up and down my back for a long while.

Time passes in that pose. A minute, an hour? Who knows? Eventually, he leans to the side, reaching for his phone atop the towel.

I prop myself up to see his words.

I'm sorry. I'm messy.

I grin at him. "You aren't alone. I am, too."

His eyes search mine in the darkness before he types again. *You enjoyed it as much as I did?*

"You couldn't tell?"

One corner of his mouth lifts. *I thought so, but confirmation is nice.*

"Let's just say *enjoyed* isn't a strong enough word. I need a word with more bite."

Then both corners of his mouth kick up at once and he's all-out grinning and my heart does a nosedive straight into my stomach.

Beast without the smile is broody and handsome and compelling.

Beast with a smile?

I might not survive it.

And with that realization follows reality. I can't have this. This isn't for me. He isn't for me. The thoughts must be scrolling across my face. The delight of the past hour dies a slow death inside my heart, and Beast's smile follows suit on its heels.

He tilts his head, a question in his eyes that needs no vocalization.

I slide off him in one smooth motion and kneel on the

towel beside him. I lean my head back, focusing on the sky above. The blanket of stars is no longer soothing, but smothering.

"We shouldn't have done that."

He sits up on an elbow, watching me.

"I'm leaving. Soon. You're . . ." I swallow. "With Caroline."

He jerks up straighter, a hand on my arm, a rough shake of his head.

"I know, you aren't, like, *together* with her, yet. But you want to be."

Maybe Caroline is a weak excuse, but the full truth is harder to admit, even to myself. I'm scared. Terrified of this thing blooming between us, the strength of it. I can't fall for him only to have it all end. Better to end before it begins, before my heart is completely annihilated.

He stills. Pulls his hand away. Bends his knees, resting his elbows on them, his hands tugging through his hair. He blows out a breath and shifts his attention toward the lake, giving me his profile.

"And even if Caroline wasn't in the picture, I can't be. I'm not letting go of my goals and aspirations, as lame as they may be. It's something I need to do for myself. I gave up everything for someone else once upon a time." And there was no happy fairy-tale ending. "I'm sorry." The words are reflexive.

I'm not sorry. I would do it all over again in a heartbeat. I would do it all night long. But that's not fair to anyone, and I'm leaving and he doesn't like me that way. Well, he wasn't complaining, so maybe it's possible he *could* like me that way, but I'm leaving. Caroline is not.

Caroline lives here. Caroline Caroline Caroline. Even if we both wanted to continue whatever this is, it's not a good idea.

He belongs with Jude and Grace, and all the others. They are his self-made family and I'm a temporary blip.

He's still staring out over the water and the silence is pushing me into a mess of rambling nerves. "It was a bad idea. You have Caroline and Blue Falls and I have . . . New York. And we're friends, right? We shouldn't have let it get out of control and now you probably feel guilty and I'm an idiot and—"

He puts a hand out and rests it on my forearm. A quick touch before pulling back.

I can't read his eyes.

He stands and sticks out his hand. I take it. He tugs me to my feet and then gathers our towels and the lantern. I watch him in stupefied silence. He doesn't try to communicate. He slips the phone in his pocket. Without another glance, he heads across the beach, back toward the path.

After a few seconds, I follow.

I walk behind him on the narrow footpath. It's as silent as a tomb. More silent. The trees are more forthcoming with their feelings at this point.

Before we get too close to the tents, I stop him, reaching out and grabbing his hand to force him to a halt.

He turns partway toward me. It's even darker here under the trees, his face a mask of grey slate.

"We're still friends, right?" I keep my voice low.

He pauses for a long time, not moving.

My hand is still grasping his lax fingers. "I don't have many friends."

The words finally garner a reaction. His hand moves, a hint of a clasp, and then he releases me and nods.

That's something. I should be relieved, but the sensation isn't presenting itself. Now it doesn't matter what he says, I've made it weird.

We can't be friends. We orgasmed together. Friends don't do that. How do I fix this? My stomach ties itself into knots. My brain goes into panic mode and lands on what feels like the most reasonable next thing to say.

"Do you still want me to help you with Caroline, or is that too weird now?"

His face is inscrutable. Heavy shoulders shrug once.

See? I knew it. I made it weird. I make everything weird. *I'm the worst.*

"That's fair." My mouth is dry. I clear my throat. "We're friends, though. If you ever need anything, I'm here."

Another short nod and then he's moving back along the path, faster than before. His long strides put him farther and farther ahead of me. Once he reaches the campsite, he stops and waits. When I get close, he hands me my lantern and towel. Then he practically bolts away toward the tent he's sharing with Grace.

The Flash is a turtle compared to this guy.

Back in my tent, I stare up at the canvas top like it will give me all the answers. But it's blank, devoid of stars and explanations.

I did the right thing. So why does it feel like I've lost everything?

Chapter Fourteen

"MY DAD TOLD me he relates to Tywin Lannister. He's like, 'No, it's hard being the head of the family!' "
–Overheard at Comic-Con

The next morning, everything is perfectly normal. Except I can't quite look Beast in the eye, I barely slept, and the guilt hanging around my neck is heavier than the Eye of Agamotto.

We cook foil-wrapped eggs and sausage in the firepit, spend a couple of early morning hours on the beach—sans games—and then before lunch, everyone helps take down the campsite for the trek back to Blue Falls.

We could only stay the one night because nearly everyone has obligations back in town. Except me and Beast. We don't have to work until tomorrow night.

Beast. My heart stutters as I shove my sleeping bag into an impossibly smaller bag.

How could I have ruined everything so terribly? What

was I thinking? I stomp my feet into the dirt, hauling some of my bags out to where the guys are repacking Fitz's truck.

He's inexperienced. Naïve. I'm like the older, more experienced woman taking advantage of—

My brain short-circuits as Beast lifts the camp box and the cooler stacked together in one mighty heft, the muscles in his shoulders bunching under his shirt.

Okay. Maybe he can't really be taken advantage of, but still. I shouldn't have instigated a sexual situation with him. Or continued it. Or brought it to its inevitable conclusion. Not when I'm leaving. Not when it isn't fair to either of us. Now we can't be friends, despite our awkward agreement last night. It isn't possible. And it's my fault.

Last night.

Memories of his hands on my breasts, teasing my nipples with his wide thumbs, send an avalanche of heat rushing through me.

"Are you okay?" Reese frowns. "You look flushed."

"I'm fine." I toss my camp gear down and race back to my tent before my traitorous face gives everything away.

I attempt to take down the tent on my own, tugging at the stakes someone has pummeled into the ground with supreme, immovable force. I take out all my aggression in my attempts to pull the items from the earth, but it's useless. I'm weak and pathetic.

And then Beast is next to me, reaching down, pulling the offensive item out with little more than a tug.

I take a few deep breaths and watch him yank out the remaining stakes like he's done this a thousand times.

I focus my gaze in the direction of the campsite, but I can't see the others from here, although occasional bits of conversation and laughter reach me through the trees.

And then Beast is in front of me.

He gives me the sign for *okay*, his pointer and thumb creating a circle while the remaining fingers are lifted up, a question in his eyes.

"I'm okay," I say, my voice whisper-soft.

And then without warning, his arms are around me and I'm surrounded by the most overwhelming and somehow tender embrace I've ever received. It lasts a second, maybe two, and then he pulls back, his hands still on my shoulders.

Our eyes lock and he smiles.

It's a forced smile. Doesn't quite reach his eyes. Nothing like the beauty he revealed last night on the beach, but . . . it's something. And because of that, I know it will all be okay.

Not the same, not even close to what my heart and body demand. But it will be okay.

"Granny, we're home!" Grace calls out as we thump into the house, unloading our bags in the entry.

It's quiet and empty. Just the ticking of the old cuckoo clock in the corner.

"Maybe she's out in the barn." My eyes alight on something bright and red hanging on the banister.

Grace's footsteps tap away toward the kitchen and I

head to the stairs, reaching for the item just as I realize what it is.

It's a bra. It's lacy and red. And it's not mine. It can't be Grace's. Only Granny has the rack for it. Grace's plodding footsteps stop and then increase in volume. She's coming this way. I snatch the red piece of lingerie, hiding it behind my back as I face her.

"What was that?" she asks.

"What? Nothing."

One hip juts out and her hand rests on it. "Why are you hiding a bra?"

"I'm not hiding anything."

"You suck at lying. Fine." She ducks around me and grabs it before I can blink. "Holy crap, who's is that?"

"Uh. Mine."

She snorts. "Your boobs are not that big. Is that Granny's? Why is it down here?"

I snatch it back. "It's none of our business."

"I can't believe Granny has a boyfriend. So that's where she's been disappearing to almost every night." Her eyes gleam as they meet mine. "We should spy on her."

"No spying."

I run up the stairs.

Grace stomps up behind me. "Oh, come on. I bet it's old Mr. Thompson. She says she doesn't like bald men but she's always telling him what to do. I think she likes bossing him around." She gasps and the sound is so loud I stop on the middle of the stairs and turn to check on her.

"What?" I ask.

She's halted on the step, eyes wide, hand on her chest. "Maybe she bosses him around in the bedroom," she whispers, lifting her brows with mock horror. I roll my eyes and keep going up the stairs while she bursts into laughter behind me. "You should see your face."

I toss the offending garment through Granny's door and it lands on the floor somewhere with a whisper of fabric.

Time for a subject change.

"I'm showering first!" I holler and beeline to the bathroom, but Grace is closer and hustles inside, shutting the door on my face before I can stop her.

"You suck!" I yell.

Her response is loud laughter. "I'll be fast."

"Yeah right." I head downstairs. I'll find Granny while I'm waiting three years for the shower.

She's out back in the shade of the awning, relaxing in a rocking chair, feet up on the patio table, smoking something that definitely isn't a cigarette.

I clear my throat and her feet whip down, hand shoving the joint down under her chair in a delayed attempt to hide it.

"Granny," I say, ready to give her the same lecture the doctor gave her at her last appointment.

"Oh, hey Fred girl." She's all innocent smiles. "Glad you made it back. Earlier I was feeling a little," she coughs, "afflicted, you know, stressed out. And it's not good to make my blood pressure rise, doctor's orders. So we should make sure we don't talk about anything . . . troubling."

"Uh-huh." This is her way of avoiding the topic. So I move on to the next. "I found your bra on the banister."

"Hmmm." She's still stubbing out her joint under the chair and pretending like I can't see it.

"I put it in your room."

"That's mighty kind of you, Fred girl. Are you hungry? I'm smoking a brisket."

"That's not all your smoking," I mutter.

She gives me the stink eye and then leans back in the rocking chair. "Where's little Miss Grace?"

"In the shower."

She doesn't say anything else about the random bra left lying around and I can't ask her, now can I?

She asks about camping and I sit on the porch with her, relaying the basics. Then we discuss dinner and what needs to be done around the farm.

Behind me, inside the house, the phone rings. I don't think I've ever heard it ring. I didn't even know people still had landlines until I came here. It sits up on the wall, attached to a base. It even has a cord, like some 1990s sitcom.

"Oh, that's right," Granny says. "Someone from New York called for you. That's likely them now."

I stand. It's still ringing. "Who is it?"

"Someone for an interview. They tried your cell first. Told them you would be out of range until today."

"Was it an accounting firm?" But that interview isn't until next week.

"No, it was something else." She squints. "Some comic store or something."

Not a comic store, Comix, the restaurant chain.

Mumbling a curse, I race inside to grab the phone, which is miraculously still ringing. "Hello?"

"Hi, is this Fredericka Klein?"

"This is she." I twist the receiver away from my mouth, keeping the top part on my ear so I don't pant down the line.

"This is Amber Hoover from the Comix group. How are you doing?"

"I'm great." I am not great. This is terrible. A nightmare come to life.

"I'm so glad I was able to reach you. Do you have a few minutes to talk with us today?"

Amber sounds way too happy and upbeat. Doesn't she realize I'm dying inside? She keeps talking and I try to listen, but my heart is hammering and nerves are turning my stomach to mush. They want to interview me. Right now.

"This is just a preliminary," she says, her voice barely intelligible through the thundering of my pulse. "No pressure, just wanted to get a feel for the type of ideas you can bring to the table."

"Right, of course, no problem." I push out the words around a thick tongue. Of course I have to agree, I can hardly say no.

"So this is just a quick exercise to see what you've got and how well you can come up with ideas under pressure. For this example, let's say you have to pick one central theme for multiple venues and convince our marketing team to develop the concept. What would you use and how would you sell it?"

My mind is blank. This is impossible. This is like asking me to . . . cut down the mightiest tree in the forest with a herring.

A light bulb illuminates over my head.

"Blessed are the cheesemakers."

A confused laugh in my ear. "What?"

My heart sinks. Either I'm too nerdy even for Comix, or Comix are a bunch of posers hiring the nerd-illiterate Ambers of the world.

Ten minutes later, I hang up and barely remember the entirety of the interview. What did they ask? What did I say? Was it coherent? Who knows?

All I can recall is that Grace came into the kitchen at one point, made faces at me, and then emulated whatever I was saying in a high-pitched, shrieky voice.

What have I done?

"How did it go?" Grace asks when I swing open the door to her room. She's sitting where she usually is, at her desk, tapping away at the computer.

"Terrible." I flop backward onto her bed.

"Yeah. It sounded pretty bad."

I grab some of her pillows and press them on top of my face, groaning into the fabric.

"Those pillows bothering you?" Grace asks without turning around.

"They're not suffocating me fast enough."

She snorts. "At least mine don't have faces on them. Yours are weird."

She's referring to the *Supernatural* pillowcase Scarlett got me for Christmas. I yank one of the pillows off my face. She's still got her back to me, but she's turned her head to the side. At least my mortal demise made her move that much. "You're too young to truly understand the allure of sleeping with Jensen Ackles and Jared Padalecki under one's cheek. But I will teach you, young padawan."

"Whatever." Her attention goes back to the computer, lines of indecipherable code scrolling across the screen. Probably something nefarious that she shouldn't be doing.

I glance around the room. It was Scarlett's, once upon a time, but Grace has made it her own. It's not what one might expect from a fourteen-year-old girl. No posters on the walls, only a few pictures of her with Beast and Jude. There's one of all of us from this past Christmas. The desk is a mess of computer parts, a motherboard, CPU, an extra processing case. More stuff I couldn't identify if someone paid me.

"So what did you hear? I think I blacked out most of the conversation."

She turns her head again and scrunches her nose. "You said something about the Spanish Inquisition?"

I groan and cover my face again.

"What were you talking about?"

"They wanted an on-the-spot pitch, and I think I was trying to sell them on a chain of Monty Python–themed restaurants."

"Who?"

I groan and cover my face again. "Come on, Grace, it's a British comedy troupe. Their movies are on Netflix!"

"Yeah, sounds great. I also heard you rambling about elderberries."

I wave a hand in the air. "That's still Monty Python."

"Interesting." But her tone is flat and bored.

I sit up, the pillows tumbling onto the bed around me. "I'm awful at interviewing in person, but on the phone it's worse. I thought I was being somewhat funny, but you can't read the room over the phone. Maybe they were smiling, maybe they were making throat slashing motions, I will never know."

There's no way they are going to hire you. Delores Umbridge is back. *You have little experience and an entirely useless degree.*

I mentally flip Delores off and wallow on Grace's bed some more, listening to her clicking away.

Something nearby beeps and Grace shuffles around. Her chair squeaks. "Beast isn't coming over until after dinner. He's doing something for Jude right now, but he's staying the night because I wanted him to come with me to my appointment in the morning."

This explains why Beast stays the night and is never here when I wake up in the late mornings or early afternoons after a shift. He wakes up early to go with Grace to her appointments. It's so sweet but . . . isn't he exhausted? He's continually doing things for her and Jude, putting all their wants ahead of his own—even sleep takes a back seat.

I shake my head.

Let it go. None of my business.

"Oh. Great." I sit up. I better go . . . do something with myself. I'm probably a mess.

My tone must betray me because she cocks her head at me. "Is something going on with you guys?"

"What? No. What do you mean?" I smooth down my

hair. My voice is high and squeaky. I am terrible at prevarication.

She swivels in the chair to face me.

Uh-oh. Not good.

"This morning when we were packing up camp, I saw Beast hug you. But it was like a weird hug."

"Um, he was trying to make me feel better. About my job search. I got some other rejections. Before the other one, just now." I wince in an effort to seem upset. She's going to see right through this.

Her head tilts. "Oh. Yeah. I guess he would understand." She swivels back around and resumes her tapping.

My ears perk at this possible new information on the enigma that is Beast. "He would?"

She shrugs, still typing. "Yeah. He applied to a culinary place in Dallas last year. Got rejected."

This is news. Annabel and Reese don't know he actually applied somewhere. But it makes me wonder, would he be open to moving? Would Grace be okay with him leaving?

"He didn't try again?"

The tapping stops. "I . . . I guess not."

"Don't you think he should reapply?"

"The culinary science degree at BFU is good." She shrugs. "Besides, we like it here. It's home, and we've never had that."

Grace uses a lot of "we" speak, as if she and Beast are a unit instead of two separate people. Did she convince him not to apply anywhere else?

We're silent for a little while, Grace doing something

illegal, me trying to figure out a way to get her to drop more information.

"Beast cooked for you a lot when you were growing up?" I ask.

"Yeah. Our uncle—" The typing stops for a two-second beat. "I don't want to talk about that."

"Sorry."

She shrugs. "We didn't always know when we would get our next meal. Went to bed hungry more nights than not. But that's all in the past." She shakes it off and continues typing. "Anyway. I'm glad you and Beast are okay."

"Right." I nod. "We're fine."

"Just don't get involved with him. You aren't staying."

My stomach plummets somewhere down to the vicinity of my toes.

She doesn't turn around and there's not even a hiccup in her fingers on the keyboard as she issues the command.

I pretend my heart isn't stuttering to a halt. She's not wrong. "Nothing's happening." I swallow hard. Time for a new topic. "If you ever want to talk to someone about whatever, you know I'm here."

She scoffs. "Granny already makes me see a therapist. I don't need more coddling."

Aaand the teenager is back. "Thanks for letting me wallow. I'm going to help Granny with dinner."

She nods but says nothing, her eyes fixed on her computer, her fingers moving at the speed of light while I leave the room.

Chapter Fifteen

"MY DREAM JOB is being a driver for those shuttles from the airport."

–Overheard at Comic-Con

"Dearly beloved, we thank you for this meal and for our time together on this earth. For the grass that grows, and the crows that sing," she pauses, "thank you, Lord, for everything."

Grace's hand squeezes mine before she releases me. "Amen. Very poetic, Granny."

"Do you think so? I reckon I could write my own sermons. I should give Pastor Michael a call."

"So Granny, what did you do while we were gone?" Grace's innocent smile and fluttering eyes fool no one.

"Oh, you know, just hung around the house. Did some chorin' and all that."

"Uh-huh. You know, Granny," Grace spears some

okra with her fork, "you've been disappearing a lot after supper and I can't find you anywhere."

"I got errands to run." She fiddles with her napkin, moving it from the side of her plate to her lap.

Grace wrinkles her nose. "What errands?"

"None of your never mind. I don't need permission from anyone to have my own time, let alone from a child. Fred, pass the gravy, please. Did I mention your mother called? She wants you to call her back when you get a chance."

"Okaaay." It's Sunday, I always talk to them on Sundays. Granny knows that. "I'll call her after dinner." I hand her the gravy boat.

The change of subject doesn't deter Grace. "Nothing is open in Blue Falls past seven except the diner and Bodean's. So what kind of errands could you be running?"

Granny chews her food, taking her time to respond. "It's a card night. With my friends. Pinochle."

Grace and I exchange a glance.

"You have friends?" Grace asks.

I take a drink of water. I am not getting into this one.

Granny puts her fork down. "I'm very well liked."

"You called Miss Prudence two bricks shy of a load," Grace says.

"So?"

"You yelled it. Out loud. At church."

Granny shrugs. "It's only the truth. And it doesn't mean I'm not well liked. But no matter. Fred girl, how's the okra? Too much salt?"

Before I can answer, Grace opens her mouth to interrupt—probably with more questions—and Granny fixes her with a hard stare. "I may not have brought you into this world, but I can take you right out of it."

Grace's mouth closes with a click. Then she throws her head back and laughs.

"Death threats are what make you happy, huh?" I take a bite of mashed potatoes smothered in gravy.

Grace shrugs. "I've heard other kids' parents tell them the same thing. Never thought anyone would care enough to threaten me with bodily harm for misbehaving. Will you pass the biscuits?"

After talking to my parents and assuring them that I'm still alive, healthy, and not wasting the entirety of my life in a hick town in Texas while living off the kindness of others, I spend the rest of the night hiding from everyone in my room. Once it's dark enough, I climb out the bedroom window with a blanket and pillow.

But once I'm in my normal position, gazing up at the sky above, I don't even register the stars. Instead, images from the night before flood my mind. The kissing. The talking. The *everything else*.

I shut my eyes and attempt to banish the memories from my brain. I need something else to think about.

Grace's words at dinner come to mind. I recognize her badgering of Granny for what it is: a test. She presses Granny to the breaking point to see how she'll respond. With discipline? With banishment? Or worse, with nothing at all? But Granny cares. She won't kick Grace out. Granny won't be sending Grace away no matter how badly she behaves—fake threats of violence notwithstanding.

My childhood was like growing up in Themyscira compared to hers. I am the luckiest person, with every opportunity, every privilege thrust at me like it's mana raining from the sky. Parents who are always there, an education I didn't have to work too hard for, food always on the table, and a roof over my head whenever I need it.

And yet here I am, moping about my lack of job prospects and life problems. The reality is hard to stomach, but necessary. The only thing that's ever really held me back is my own dumb decisions.

This revelation is still slopping shame all over me when the window below opens and there's a gentle tap on my foot.

I sit up, wrapping my arms around my legs. Over the edge of the roof, Beast's head appears.

Not like a disembodied head or anything. His head is followed by his shoulders and the rest of his large form, hauling himself up onto the roof in one smooth movement. He sits next to me, taking up most of the small space.

"What are you doing?"

He pulls his phone out of his back pocket and types into it before showing me the screen. *Checking on you.*

A laugh huffs out of me. Of course. "Who checks on you?"

He freezes.

"Never mind. I'm stargazing while I can, because once I go back . . ." I trail off on a shrug.

We sit side by side in silence for long minutes. Despite last night, it's not uncomfortable like I might have expected, even though we're basically in the same position as we were when things went haywire. Sexy haywire.

He taps something out on his phone and shows it to me.

Did you tell your parents about the job interview today?

My head snaps up. "Did Grace blab? I'm gonna put toothpaste in her shampoo bottle."

I swear his mouth turns up, but it's hard to see for sure in the moonlight.

"I didn't tell them. It was too embarrassing." And if Grace is going to spill my secrets, I don't feel so bad about spilling what she revealed. "Grace told me you applied to a culinary school in Dallas."

He's still again. Then he types, *I didn't get in.*

"You could apply again. You know, there's a really good one in New York. The Culinary Institute of America, the CIA. Wouldn't it be pretty badass to tell people you go there?"

Can't leave Grace and Jude. They're my only family. You have your parents, I have them.

"I get it." Though I don't like it. Why can't they move for him if he would stay for them?

Blue Falls might not be the best, but it's something. Maybe I'll open a restaurant someday or maybe I'll take over your job at Bodean's when you leave.

"Usurper," I accuse. Then I nudge him with my elbow. "It's an assistant type job, but Lucas is talented. And you would be good at it."

Maybe.

"Why wouldn't you be?"

He huffs out a breath. Points at his mouth.

"That's not an impediment. Most people talk too much, and then they don't shut up and ramble out nonsense."

I'm not sure I've met anyone that meets that description.

"Hardy har har."

I can't see his face in the dim light, just the edge of his profile limned in moonlight. I wish I could make him understand his own potential. I can't let him make the same mistakes I made.

"Because of Jack, I put aside all of my aspirations or thoughts of doing anything for myself. No." I shake my head. "That's not right, because of *myself*, I made the awful decision to put Jack first. The problem was he was putting Jack first, too. I put everything into our relationship. If I had made myself a priority, or recognized my own value and had the strength to stand up for myself, I wouldn't be here."

He jabs his phone with hard fingers. *Jack was an idiot.*

"Agreed."

Even a friend wouldn't ask you to give things up for them.

"You're probably right. But it was my fault, too. Don't make my mistakes. Beast, I care about you and I want you to put you first."

It's not that easy.

He's typing again, so I'm watching over his shoulder when his phone lights up with an incoming text.

I can't wait to see you!!! Where are you taking me on our first date? You should pick somewhere we get to dress up!! Or maybe go dancing!!!

Followed by heart eye emoji and a woman dancing in a red dress emoji.

The words are as welcome as a screw twisting in my stomach.

In the dim light, his jaw is hard and unsmiling. What is he thinking? He's not the type to go for a fancy dinner and dancing. I don't know how I know that, but I just do. Having to talk to people, order food, drive Caroline somewhere while she bears the brunt of holding up their conversation and all that considering they barely know each other . . .

But I can't tell what's going through his mind. He stares at the phone. Then he switches over to the notepad app. *Maybe I should break it off.*

My response is automatic, even though it kills me to say it, the words like spitting shards of glass. "No. Don't do that. We'll figure something else out that's not so . . . complicated. Something she'll enjoy that you're comfortable with, too."

He pauses for a long moment, head tilted back, staring up at the sky. He's a statue of tension for a full minute before he takes a breath and types again.

You think she'll be open to an alternate suggestion?

"Probably. She clearly likes you a lot." I can't believe I'm defending her. The last thing I want is to see her hanging all over Beast at work, but that isn't fair. We may be diametrically opposed foes, but Beast's happiness is more important to me than my own vicious jealousy.

There are other issues.

"What do you mean?"

I've noticed she can be . . . rude. Not to me, but to others.

"You mean at Bodean's."

He nods.

"Yeah, I've served her before. But she was with her friends and probably distracted. Besides, I'm a Yank and sometimes the Southern hospitality is so overdone it all feels condescending. I'm used to New Yorkers yelling at me on the street for getting into the taxi they wanted. Not all that 'bless your heart' when it really means you're an ass."

His lips twitch, but he's distracted, his gaze glued to the phone. He flips back over to the text conversation and stares at it, fingers unmoving.

"Tell her you'll plan a surprise. Then you can get all dressed up and make her a fancy meal yourself with your mad cooking skills. You can plan for it somewhere romantic, but you won't have to try and communicate with other people and make it complicated. It'll be great." I force enthusiasm into my tone, but the words are strained.

He follows my direction and is rewarded with even more exclamation points and emojis.

Yep. It will be super-duper great.

I've got a front row seat to Beast's love life, a demise of my own making. Every text, every piece of advice, every question on how to be with her, they're all like the sharpest of filleting knives, slicing a little further.

Thank you for helping me.

Slice.

Chapter Sixteen

YES, that is Love—that wind
Of terrible and jealous beauty, blowing
Over me—that dark fire, that music . . .
–Cyrano de Bergerac

The kitchen is so hot, I'm seriously contemplating whether I can fit in the freezer.

"Lucas. My boob sweat is turning into Wakanda Falls."

He presses his lips together, shaking his head. "Does that mean it's challenge day?"

Surprised, I laugh. "I'll let you know if I ascend the throne."

I can't believe he got the reference. Last week I dropped a glass in the bar area and said, "Dammit, Janet." Eliza gave me a weird look and asked, "Who's Janet?"

How does anyone go their whole lives without a little *Rocky Horror*?

I finish sanitizing the cutting board I was using and then take out the trash, enjoying all the most glamorous aspects of working in a kitchen.

"I'll be right back," I call before running out the door. There's a slight lull—Tuesday nights aren't as bad as the rest of the week—so I don't feel too bad about leaving Lucas to suffer alone.

But I almost run right back into hell's kitchen as soon as I exit. Just as I'm making my way to the back, at the front door, Caroline jumps all over Beast like a hyperactive puppy.

She must have just arrived.

Wincing, I avert my eyes and race down the back hallway, past the public bathrooms and Ranger's office and out into the night air. I chuck the garbage in the bin and slam the lid down. And then wait.

So it's not normally where I like to spend my time. It's barely cooler here than it is in the kitchen, and it smells like old food and ass, but I can't go back in there and watch Beast with Caroline. I just can't.

It's been a week since the campout, and Beast and I have settled back into our nice, normal, friendly routine. And I hate it. He hasn't asked me to help him with Caroline anymore, but I know they've been texting. And now, she's back. And she's here.

After I've dawdled as long as possible, I make my way back inside. At least dealing with the heat in the kitchen is better than being stuck at the bar and watching the Beast and Caroline show.

"I've got it covered," Lucas says as soon as he sees me. "But the bar is busy. Eliza wants help."

"Great." Perfect. Wonderful. I can do this. I just won't let my eyes stray to the front door. Problem solved.

My plan is working out to perfection. I stay busy hustling drinks behind the bar for about an hour. But then . . .

"Um, excuse me? Bartender? I asked for three cherries and there's only two."

Caroline. She's leaning against the end of the bar, glaring at me like I peed in her drink instead of forgetting one small itty-bitty little cherry.

"Sorry about that." I use a bright blue, sword-shaped cocktail pick and stab a cherry from the dish behind the counter. I reach over to put it in her drink.

She pulls the glass back before I can drop it in. "Uh, excuse me, I would like you to make me another drink."

I tilt my head. "You want another of the same or something different?"

"I want the drink I ordered, made correctly this time. And I shouldn't have to pay for any of it." Then she puts the martini glass to her lips and takes a long sip, eyeing me over the rim.

"Um. I'm confused. You want to drink that one," I point the skewered cherry at her, "but you also want a new one? And you don't want this cherry?" I hold it up. "And you want it all free?"

"Do you not speak English?"

My jaw clenches against a snarky retort. But something slips out anyway. "*BIlugh 'e' DaHar'a'*," I say, which literally translates into *you're a dumb twat* in Klingon.

She frowns. "What?"

I hesitate. I can't exactly keep insulting the customers, even in fictional languages. "Your request is irrational and you're a condescending harpy." Oops. Guess I insulted her in her native language.

Her mouth pops open in outrage but before she can respond, I'm saved.

"Oh, Beast." Caroline's entire demeanor morphs from insulting shrew to bubbly coed when he stops next to her. "Is it your break time now?" Her voice is all bright, smooth notes flavored with innocence.

He nods.

"I'll go with you." She dimples up at him and one corner of his mouth inches upward.

And suddenly I want to stab myself with the cocktail sword. He smiled at her. A small one, but still.

Jealousy twists and tangles itself into knots in my stomach. I want to She-Hulk Smash.

My face must show some emotion because Beast watches me, brow furrowing.

I huck the cherry in the trash. "I'll grab you some food from the kitchen. Be there in a sec." Eliza is at the other end of the bar with a customer. "Be right back," I yell.

In the kitchen, I plate up the special, crawfish étouffée, and then cut a hunk of freshly baked french bread and throw it on top.

I will bring Beast his food. Smile. Act normal. Show them that everything is okay and I don't care if Beast smiles at a blonde parasite who makes Lex Luthor seem like a philanthropist. A parasite I helped set him up with.

But there's no chance for nonchalance. I push open

the door to the office and freeze, rendered immobile by a surge of dread edged with panic.

Beast is sitting on the couch, Caroline next to him. But that's not what has me wanting to vomit. Caroline is leaning over *kissing* Beast, her lips grazing one corner of his mouth. Though by the time the door has swung fully open, he's yanked away from her.

She pulls back, blinking rapidly. "Oh."

What the hell?

"Here's your food." I put the plate on the table and turn back, bolting out of the room and shutting the door firmly behind me.

I stand there for a few, heartbreaking seconds. The rapid beat inside my chest constricts my breath. I can't get enough air. I make it as far as the kitchen but then stop outside the door, hiding in the little alcove by the swinging doors. I can't go back out to the bar like this.

Even while my body is spiraling in panic, my mind cycles through emotions, trying to make sense of it. I am being ridiculous. He's not mine to pine over. I'm leaving. I'm not staying here. There is nothing for me here. I can't live in Blue Falls and work at Bodean's for the rest of my life. It's not meant to be. Besides, he wants Miss Caroline Perfect Pout. Not Piranha-Face-Fred. It's okay for him to go after her. I have no rights to this overreaction. I'm the one who told him we were a mistake.

My eyes are screwed shut, heart pounding in my ears, so when a gentle touch lands on my arm I almost leap out of my skin.

"Beast," I breathe.

He points at me, then makes the okay sign. *You okay?*

"I'm fine."

He tugs on my arm, gentle but firm. Two hard shakes of his head. His eyes are locked on to me, his jaw a hard edge of granite. A muscle twitches in his cheek and then he mouths, *Not fine. Lying.*

"It's . . . we can't talk now. I'll tell you later, okay?" I turn to flee. I've got to get back to the bar.

He stops me, a hand on my shoulder. His brow is creased, eyes troubled, blinking, his breath coming in short pants between parted lips. I don't think I've ever seen him in this state. Oddly, the reaction soothes my own whirling emotions.

He points a hard finger at me, then makes a talking motion with his thumb and fingers, open and shut.

You. Talk.

I grab his titan hand and give it a squeeze. "Beast. Everything will be fine, I promise. I can't do this right now. I have to get to work. But I swear we'll talk later. Okay?" I stalk away before he can respond, not looking back.

Back at the bar, I throw myself into work, taking orders, mixing drinks, restocking the beer cooler, trying to get my mind off the vision in the office. I can't think about it or I might hurt someone. Someone blonde.

After I help Eliza catch up, I wait on a couple of tables that have filled. I'm at the bar, waiting for Eliza to put the last drink on the tray, when she asks me, "What's up with Beast?"

"There's nothing happening with me and Beast."

She laughs. "I didn't ask— You know what, never mind. Will you slice more limes when you're done bringing these drinks to table nine?" She puts the drink on a tray.

Keeping busy is a good idea. I can't get the image of Caroline out of my head. Leaning toward him. Kissing him. Her lips on his skin. I used to be the last person he'd kissed. The only one. Now it's Caroline.

And I thought she was nice and normal and good for Beast. Pfft.

Once I drop off the drinks at table nine and bus a few empties, I grab a bag of limes and a chef's knife.

It's rather satisfying, slicing through the hard citrus and chunking the results into the garnish holder.

"What did that lime ever do to you?" Eliza asks, a laugh in her voice.

"You asked me to cut them." Slam. Slam. Slam.

"I can see that. Very exuberantly. I like your enthusiasm."

Somehow, I make it through the rest of the shift. Somehow, I only glance twice—maybe three times—at the front where Beast is manning the door. Somehow, I don't scream at the top of my lungs every time Caroline reaches over to touch Beast. Somehow, I don't throw the knife at Eliza when Beast is stacking chairs at the end of the night and she casually mentions she purchased him a size too-small on purpose. I have to grind my teeth, but I get through it. Time moves inexorably forward. And then finally it's over.

But with that realization comes a new wave of anxiety. I have to talk to Beast. Tell him why I'm upset.

How do I explain that I want to be around him all the time? That I want to know everything about him? That I don't want any other women touching him or kissing him? I'm a total psycho.

Beast is outside in the front lot with Caroline while I lag behind, taking too long to say good night to the others.

I know I can't avoid him forever, but I'm hoping to avoid witnessing the inevitable good-night kiss with Caroline. Or worse. What if he drops me off at Granny's and leaves to meet up with her?

I walk out with Lucas but stop on the front porch.

Lucas keeps walking. "You and Beast drive careful." He looks up at the sky and then back at me. "Storms a'comin."

"Okay. You, too."

He waves a hand and gets in his car.

On the other side of the parking lot, Beast is at his truck, leaning against the driver's door, Caroline standing in front of him.

They hug. My heart twists. Caroline kisses his cheek. My stomach revolts.

Then she leaves. She gets into her vehicle and pulls out behind Lucas.

I force my gaze back to Beast.

He's watching me. Thunder booms in the distance. He jerks his head at his truck and then gets in without waiting for me.

Up in the dark sky, the stars are concealed by clouds.

I glance around, looking for Storm and the rest of the X-Men, but it's just me and Beast and this ridiculous cliché of a storm settling a sense of foreboding deep in my gut.

Chapter Seventeen

"THIS IS the only time that it's cool to be a geek."
—Overheard at Comic-Con

The first drops of rain patter around me, tapping my shoulder, striking my cheek. I slam the door shut and the smattering becomes a deluge. Sheets of water slide down the windows, surrounding the quiet warmth of the truck.

Beast kicks the windshield wipers into high gear and we drive in silence, but not for long. After a few minutes, he parks under the same tree where we first kissed, shoving the truck into park and clicking it off.

I stare out the windshield while rain drenches the leaves above, the tree only providing a hint of resistance as water hammers all around us.

He watches me. Waiting.

I can't look at him when I say it, but I owe him the truth. I keep my gaze on the night and try to swallow through the nerves threatening to explode out of my jittering limbs.

"I didn't like seeing Caroline kiss you." I take a deep breath and hold it.

He's not saying anything. Not moving. I risk a quick glance. He's facing me, but his expression is hard and flat.

"Because I was jealous, okay?" The words spill out of me like water onto a comic book, bleeding colorful ink. "I know it's stupid. I know it's highly illogical. I know that I'm leaving soon and it's unfair and I can't expect—"

He slides across the bench seat, cutting my words off with the press of his mouth. The kiss is brutal, hard, and all too brief.

He pulls back an inch to look into my face. His arm is along the back of the seat, the other one near my leg, not touching me, but nearly. I can't do anything but stare at him.

My heart is pounding its way out of my ribcage. My shirt is probably vibrating with the force of it, but I can't look down to check because I'm pinned under Beast's dark eyes.

"But Caroline."

He shakes his head.

"No?" I try to interpret the motion. "No more Caroline?"

He leans away far enough to pull out his phone. *I told her we should be friends.*

My hands clench in my lap. "Is that what I saw in the parking lot?"

He nods, and now he's wary, watchful.

"Oh."

Oh.

"But." I swallow against the sand in my mouth. "What does this mean? What about . . . you know . . . I'm still leaving?"

Shrugs.

"You don't care?"

Types. *I care.*

He presses another surprise kiss to my mouth, not as brutal as the last. Tender this time.

Then he's typing again. *You're here now.*

"Yeah, but once I'm gone . . . what if you wanted to," the words have to be forced out, "start something up with Caroline and I've ruined your chances?"

Typing quickly. *I don't like Caroline. I like you.*

"But—"

He huffs before I can continue my line of thought and then he's typing again. *I never really wanted to be with Caroline.*

Wait. What? "You didn't?"

It's always been you.

My stomach unknots itself and backflips about forty times.

He stops typing. Eyes flick to mine. *But I didn't think I had a shot.*

"Then why did you ask me to help you with Caroline?" My voice is quiet and confused. I'm surprised he can hear me over the pounding of the rain.

I thought you and I could just be friends and she was safer.

"Safer?" My world is shattered. No, not shattered, *transformed*, like Doctor Strange transmuting a gun into a swarm of flies.

She was interested in me. You weren't. I didn't have cause to hope until the lake, and then

He stops typing and we lock eyes. He shrugs.

My mind plays over our time at the lake. The hot decadence on the beach followed by my own insistence that we remain friends. I rejected him, just like he thought I would.

"I'm still not safer."

I've decided to live dangerously.

A surprised laugh startles out of me. "I guess I've been playing it safe, too. But I like you. I think I've liked you from the beginning and I didn't want to admit it to myself. Because I can't repeat the same mistakes I made with Jack."

I don't want you to give up anything for me. I'm not Jack.

"I know you're not." Even though part of me wishes he would ask me to give it up for him. But he's right, he's not Jack. He wouldn't ask it of me, and I won't do it. And I can't be the Jack in his life. I can't ask him to give up Grace and Jude, his life in Blue Falls for me.

"So. I guess we're doing this. Whatever *this* is."

He smiles. A slow grin that moves across his face and takes my breath away.

I lift a hand, wanting to touch the pleasure revealing itself on his face. Before my fingers make contact, he grabs my wrist, turning his head to set a kiss on my palm. The move is affectionate and arousing. There's still a trace of a smile on his face when I lean forward and capture the hint of joy, this time with my mouth.

He doesn't stop me and we spend endless minutes exploring each other with lips, tongues, fingertips.

When I straddle his thighs, dipping to avoid knocking my head on the ceiling, I praise the powers that be for creating bench seats. His arms surround me, and I'm wrapped up in him, content and secure. His hands tug through my hair, pulling out the ponytail, sending my hair cascading around us and cradling my head in his hands while we kiss and play, tender and turned on all at the same time.

Throbbing desire weaves its spell around us, expanding like a thick cloud. I pull back before we can get sucked in too far.

"Will you tell me your real name?"

He spells it out with his hand. *G-E-O-R-G-E.*

"George?" I laugh, meeting his gaze. "That's—wait, no." I gasp, clutching at his hand.

He tugs on a strand of my hair, eyes worried, then lifts his hands in a *what?* gesture.

"That makes us Fred and George."

He tilts his head, eyes narrowed.

"We're basically the Weasley twins."

His eyes widen and then his mouth is twitching.

"Okay, no. We can't make out now." I slap his arms in frustration. "They're brothers. This is all wrong."

His head drops to my shoulders. He's shaking. I put a hand on him. "George? Are you . . . laughing?"

A discordant rumble emerges from his throat.

"You *are* laughing!" I accuse.

His head lifts, his smile wider than the Texas sky.

"You have a dimple." I touch his cheek with the tip of my finger. His smile gets somehow bigger.

"It's huge. But of course it is, it has to match the rest of you. I bet I could stick my fist in that thing."

He's laughing again, a strange, rusty hum, and it makes me laugh, too, and then his hands are on my shoulders and he's capturing my laugh inside of his.

And just like every time we've kissed, my whole body ignites with restless need, yearning for more. And the affliction must get Beast, too, because our mouths crash together with ever-increasing aggression. It's like a competitive sport to see who can kiss who with more enthusiasm.

But he never attempts to push it further.

When I reach for his zipper, he brings the kiss to an end, pecking me one last time before leaning back slightly. His lips are swollen and his eyes are hooded with unmet desire.

"Why are we stopping?"

He holds up a finger and reaches for his phone, which has fallen onto the floor. I have to hold on to his shoulders while he leans over and stretches to search. Settling my head closer, I nibble his neck a little. He shivers and comes back with his phone. I straighten, moving back to give him room but my head hits the ceiling. He helps shift me off his lap, then tugs me against his side.

I want to make sure we're exclusive. You can't be teaching anyone else how to kiss.

"I'm not the one with a cute blonde vying for my attention at Bodean's every night," I grumble.

He smiles.

I halfheartedly hit him in the shoulder. "It's not funny."

So I'm your boyfriend now?

"I . . . yes? Is that what you want?"

He nods.

I bite my lip. Grace isn't going to be happy about this. "Are we telling the others? Granny? Grace?"

Why wouldn't we?

"Grace told me to not get involved with you."

He nods again, unsurprised. *She's worried about you leaving.*

"Yeah, she loves you. She's protecting your heart." I put my hand on his chest, just to feel the warmth and strength and beat of it under my fingers.

He shakes his head no.

"No?"

He types. *She might be worried about me, but she will hurt when you leave, too.*

"Ouch," I say. I haven't even considered how Grace might feel about my departure. "I don't want to hurt her. Or you or anyone."

Sometimes it can't be helped. Life is pain, highness.

I smile at that. "Nice reference." I lean back, needing more than a few inches of space to process this conversation. The thought of leaving is akin to gripping the sharp edge of a blade on purpose. A self-inflicted wound not easily managed. And it's only going to get worse.

Beast runs a finger down my cheek, then holds up his phone.

It won't be goodbye. It will be see you later.

"I hope so."

A light caress of his fingers down my arm to my hands, then he links one hand with mine.

"Are you sure you want to do this with me? Since I'm not a safe bet?"

You're worth it.

Our eyes lock and everything in me melts into something warm and miraculous. How can he believe in me when I don't even believe in myself? Jack didn't. Even my parents don't, not really.

I grip his hand tighter. "I wish I could be as brave as you are."

I'm not brave.

"Oh, yes you are. Look at everything you do. You take care of everyone. You go to school, despite not being able to talk. You've protected Grace her whole life, taken care of her and Jude, and moved wherever they needed to go. You asked me for help. That took courage. You're here now, with me, despite the fact that I'm leaving. You might be scared, but you do it anyway. That is true bravery."

He bites his lip, considering me for a moment before typing again. *Granny has been taking me to see specialists.*

"That's a good thing."

You don't think it makes me unstable?

"What? No. Why would you . . ."

He's still typing.

I'm seeing a speech therapist, but also a psychologist. His eyes search mine, like he's worried I'm going to think he's not in his right mind.

Something warm melts inside me. "Uh, Beast. I've seen a therapist. Many times. Literally everyone I know has gone at one point or another, and most go regularly. There's nothing wrong with working on being the best version of yourself. And sometimes that means talking to someone who can listen and advise without judgment."

I haven't spoken in so long, my muscles have forgotten how. But the problem is beyond that. I have to fix my mind.

My hand tenses around his again. How could he think such a thing? "There's nothing wrong with your mind. You aren't broken. I think you're perfect just as you are. Even if you never spoke again, Beast, you would still be —" I cut myself off. Everything. He could be everything. But I can't say that, I can't even think it.

He doesn't push me to keep my train of thought going. Instead, he quirks a lip at me and then he traces his thumb over my collarbone, rubbing my skin for a moment, like he needs the contact as much as I do, and then types again.

Every time I try to talk, a lump fills my throat and it's like I can't breathe. The muscles don't matter until I can get through that wall.

I lean into him, pressing my head to his chest. The steady beat of his heart is a soothing rhythm in my ear while we both watch his phone. "I get it. And I know you can do this, if you want. I will be here to support you in any way you need. And you don't have to tell me everything."

Why did you go?

I know what he's asking without him having to clarify. "Anxiety, mostly. It can be hard for me to talk to people I don't know, or be in situations where I don't know what to expect."

He blinks, surprised. *But you're so*

He stops typing, lifts his head, shrugs, types again.

you.

"Yeah, now. I used to take medication for my anxiety. It was really bad, especially if I had to do public speaking, or anything with a lot of people. I'd freeze up, have a panic attack, it was awful. But with the help of a therapist I was able to figure out ways to manage it. I still get nervous in large crowds sometimes, but now I can recognize the signs and do things to calm myself. Take deep breaths, take time out, confront what's making me anxious, and try to break it down into manageable chunks."

He nods, watching me with those intense dark eyes, like he's memorizing my words, letting them seep into his bones. The ever-present tension gripping his shoulders slips away as I talk.

"Going to Comic-Con helped, too. Maybe because I wasn't the only geek in the room. And with fandoms . . . they make you feel like you aren't alone, you know? You're surrounded by people who aren't afraid to talk about how much they love things, nerdy things. It gives you this connection, without shame or embarrassment. If only we could all bond on such a level. The world would be a happier place."

We talk longer. I tell him about the first time my dad brought me to Comic-Con and I convinced him to dress up like Hawkeye. He tells me some funny stories about Jude's parties, but he doesn't dive into his past, and I don't push him. We share innocent touches and conversation until I'm hoarse.

"We should probably get home. The sun will be rising soon."

We disentangle our limbs and Beast starts the truck. Before he puts it in gear, he reaches over and tugs me closer, pulling me into the middle of the bench seat.

"The porch light is on," I say as we're approaching. The figure on the porch comes into focus.

Granny.

"Uh-oh."

She's sitting on the porch swing with a rifle lying across her lap.

Chapter Eighteen

SPEAK to her
Speak, man!

Through my nose? She might laugh at me;
That is the one thing in this world I fear!
–Cyrano de Bergerac

"Hey, Granny," I call out as we're exiting the truck. "It's a bit late to be shooting at rabbits."

"I'm not looking for rabbits. Looking for something a little bigger."

Beast, ever the protector, steps in front of me and blocks me from Granny's view.

"Oh, hells bells, Beast, I'm not gonna shoot either of you. This is just a warning. This here is a Christian household and there will be no shenanigans under my roof until there are rings on those fingers."

I lean around Beast to eye Granny. "Why would you think—"

"Don't even try to hide the truth. I've got eyes in the back of my skull and a few up in the clouds. I didn't fall off the turnip truck yesterday."

Beast glances down at me and shrugs.

"We promise to be good. Can we come in now? Not at gunpoint?"

She stands up, pointing the rifle at the ground. "It's fine. Beast, you best be sleeping downstairs, and Fred girl, you better not leave your room until that sun comes up or you'll both be answering to Betsy."

Betsy must be the rifle. "We promise."

Beast's hand slides into mine as Granny stalks inside, muttering something under her breath.

When she disappears from view, he leans down, sneaking a quick kiss.

"Jesus should fit between you!" Granny yells and we leap apart.

We gape at each other, wide-eyed, and then I slap my hand over my mouth to smother the laughter.

It's early afternoon when I finally wake up from the deepest slumber ever and stumble downstairs for coffee.

"Oh, luscious bringer of life," I whisper to the coffee pot, which miraculously contains a full carafe of delectable, mouthwatering brew.

"You're welcome," Granny says, walking into the kitchen and standing next to me.

Grabbing a mug from the cupboard, I pour myself a cup and face her, leaning my butt against the counter. "Thanks, you." I lift my mug in cheers and take a careful sip.

"What's going on with you and the big fella?"

"Cutting straight to the point, I see."

She lifts her brows, unimpressed.

"Is he here?"

"He left earlier, had an appointment in town. Answer the question, Fred girl."

I take another sip before responding. "I like him. We're . . . together." I shrug, not sure how to explain it when I can't quite wrap my own head around it.

"You're not staying here."

My heart jumps and I stand up straight. "Are you kicking me out?"

She rolls her eyes and moves closer. "Don't be slow, girl. That's not what I'm talking about. I mean you have plans. You aren't staying in Blue Falls. Beast belongs here."

And I don't. "I know."

"Do you?"

"It's nothing, Granny."

"I reckon it's more than nothing. You have a good heart. It's already bruised. I'd hate to see it torn."

I put the coffee down on the counter. I can't do anything but nod due to the massive lump in my throat. *It's too late.*

It's like she hears the words anyway. She hugs me, surrounding me with the smell of Chanel No. 5 and pipe tobacco. Surprisingly, not a bad combo.

"You're not in trouble. I'm not mad at you." She pulls back, keeping one hand on each of my shoulders. "Can't say I blame you either. That boy is mighty fine. If only I was ten years younger."

A surprised laugh barks out of me. "*Ten* years younger?"

"That's what I said." She steps back, hands on her hips, squinting at me. "Ten years. Did I stutter? Lost your hearing?"

Through sheer force of will I keep my face blank. "Right, right. Ten years." I salute. "I hear you."

"Will you clean out the shed today? I think there's an old bicycle in there. I want to get it fixed up for Grace as a surprise."

"Oh, cool. Yeah, absolutely."

Granny leaves for parts unknown and I've only had a few more sips of coffee when Grace bounces in.

"You got an email. I think it's from that interview on Monday." She puts the laptop on the counter.

Too soon. It's gotta be bad news. "Are you hacking my emails again?"

"It's not hacking when your password for everything is 'I love Jensen Ackles.' " She sighs and rolls her eyes.

"I use numbers and characters, too." I stare at the laptop on the counter, not quite ready to open it. My stomach swirls with nerves. "Well? What did the email say?"

She disappears behind an open cabinet, rooting for snacks. "I didn't read it. I just saw the sender and subject. I'm not a monster."

"The truth of that statement has yet to be determined." I bite my lip. I want to read it, but I know the odds of receiving good news are slim to none. My interview was terrible. My major qualification is being a giant nerd who also loves food but struggles with simple conversation. I want this job, it's perfect. But if I get it, it will likely mean leaving Blue Falls within the next couple of weeks and Beast . . .

I shove the thought away. I've got a month or less, either way.

I stare at the laptop, closed on the countertop, mocking me with its sleek simplicity. "Maybe I'll read it after my chores."

"Don't be a big baby." Leaving the cabinet door open, she walks across the kitchen to the fridge and peers inside.

I can't believe I'm caving to pressure from a semi-adult who doesn't even know how to close cabinet doors or take less than three hours to shower. But I am.

I open the laptop and sign into my email account.

Dear applicant,

We regret to inform you . . .

"I didn't get it." And *Dear applicant*? Really? Reduced to a generic form letter.

"Are you kidding me? They are stupider than stupid!" Grace slams the fridge shut and opens the freezer, grabbing a pint of ice cream.

"I think I'm the stupid one in this situation."

I knew I didn't have a shot, but a huge part of me is still crushed by the rejection. This was literally a once-in-a-lifetime dream job. Another, smaller part of me is relieved to be able to stay in Blue Falls a little longer. Then I'm angry at myself for even wanting to stay longer at all. I won't be the old Fred who lets go of her dreams.

Grace hops up on the counter, digging into the ice cream. "At least it means you can stay longer."

I walk over and put a hand on her shoulder. "You know, I have to move back eventually, but we'll always be friends. No matter where I'm living. You're like the little sister I never wanted."

Grace snorts out a laugh and pokes at her ice cream with a fork.

"Why do you always use a fork with ice cream? It's not natural."

She shrugs and swallows. "I like it this way."

"Well, when I move back to New York and have a swanky apartment—which means my room will at least be bigger than a closet—you can come stay with me."

The fork lowers and her eyes widen. "You mean it?"

"Of course. As long as it's okay with Granny and everyone. We would have so much fun. You'd love Coney Island. And in the big city, I can teach you how to use a spoon like a normal human."

She rolls her eyes, lets out a beleaguered sigh, and grabs a tiny bite with her fork. "Are you going to apply for more jobs?"

"I have my résumé out to a bunch of places, but yeah. I should keep looking."

The thought of schlepping my résumé to more places, places I don't really want to work anyway, makes my heart sink into my stomach. I highly doubt I'll find anything as good as a nerdy chain of restaurants comprised of everything I love.

Grace is frowning down into her ice cream tub, poking at it with her fork. A flash of affection trips through me. It's sweet that she cares.

"Hey." I nudge her with my shoulder. "I'll apply for jobs that will build up my résumé so the next time Comix has an opening, I'll be even more perfect and they can't possibly refuse me."

Grace meets my eyes, then smiles slowly and nods. "I'll help you search."

We spend the afternoon in Grace's room. She even helps me complete auto forms and submit my résumé on her computer while I use the laptop and we get double the applications done.

Before leaving for work, I give her an impulsive hug. "Hey. Thanks for helping me today."

She pats me on the back with two sharp taps. "No sweat."

Work is much less stressful without Caroline. And every time I leave the kitchen and peer at the door, Beast is there all beefy and brutally handsome. Knowing he's all mine makes wings take flight in my stomach. Nothing as tame as butterflies, we're talking full on pterodactyls.

During his break, I bring him dinner to the office, as per usual.

Except this time after I set his plate on the table, he yanks me down into his lap and kisses me senseless.

Then his hands move. *I miss you.*

"Really? You miss me? I'm literally within a hundred yards of you, like, every second of the day."

His head tilts on a grin, then he lands a quick kiss on my neck, inciting a shiver down my spine.

"You miss kissing me," I deduce.

The smile turns mischievous. He nods.

"Same, Beast, same. But I gotta get back. And you only have a few more minutes to eat."

I try for one last hurried graze of lips, but instead of a quick goodbye, it morphs into a full-blown make out. After a few minutes, I pry myself off him. Not because he's holding on too tight, but because I don't want to go.

The rest of the shift takes a million years. I could have watched *Avengers: Endgame* three times before the clock finally hits one and Eliza hollers for last call.

Time continues to move at a snail's pace but then finally, *finally*, we're walking out together.

He opens the passenger door, but before I can climb in, he's leaning into my space, and his mouth covers mine. We kiss for long enough that I lose track of where I am until a wolf whistle pierces the air.

"Get it, girl!" Eliza yells.

The others are walking to their cars, laughing and clapping.

Beast doesn't immediately release me. Instead, he gives me one last biting kiss before jogging around to the other side to get in.

"Well, that was embarrassing."

Shameless, Beast shrugs and offers me a hint of a smile, but the smug satisfaction is clear even in the small movement.

"You enjoyed that, didn't you?"

He nods.

"I didn't take you for someone who would be into public displays of affection."

His head tilts and points at me, then signs, *Only you.*

My breath catches. "We don't have to go back to the ranch yet, right?'

He stares at me for a long second and then starts the truck. He tugs me into his side, waiting until I've buckled in with the middle belt before pulling out of the lot.

The heat of his palm sears my leg while he drives one-handed.

He parks us under the tree again, in what I now consider to be our spot.

There's a heated pause as we both stare out the window at the tree. His hand clenches on my leg and I face him.

"Beast."

He looks at me.

And then we're kissing. His tongue strokes against mine, his hand clenching my leg. I trace my fingers up the corded muscles of his arm and tug at his shirt.

"Take this off." The command is breathless and he immediately complies. I unbutton my blouse but then stop when his chest is exposed to the subtle lights of the dash, my gaze fixed on each curve and valley lined with heavy muscle.

Beast brushes aside my frozen fingers, unbuttoning my shirt for me while I continue to admire his masculine beauty, tracing him with my eyes and then my fingers, the heat of his skin swamping me with hunger.

I shrug out of my blouse. His gaze is a hot stroke as I unhook my bra and toss it somewhere on the floor.

His eyes spark with restrained passion. He signs, *Show me.*

"Show you what?"

What you like.

I grasp one big hand and pull it up to my breast. "You already know some of what I like." I encourage him to hold me, and he takes over with slow strokes of his fingers.

Our breathing is loud and ragged, filling the small cab.

He leans down and takes one nipple into his mouth with a soft suck. The pleasure is almost painful.

"Beast." I couldn't stop the moan if I tried. I should be embarrassed at my own need, but I don't even care. "More."

He immediately pulls away.

"No." I reach for him, but his focus is on unbuttoning my pants. I help him yank them off and then he's staring down at my simple yellow panties like he's Indiana Jones and they're the Holy Grail.

Show me, he signs again.

I lie there trying not to combust for maybe three seconds, catching my breath. Tired of waiting, he picks up my hand and puts it between my legs.

I chuckle at his stern expression but I'm too turned on to deny him, or myself, this pleasure. Especially when my eyes drop from his face to the erection straining his pants. I lick my lips and his breath falters. I rub myself through the thin fabric of my underwear and his breathing gets even more jagged.

"Beast." His name is a moan. "Touch me."

He shifts on the seat, leaning closer to where my fingers move faster, but he doesn't follow my command.

I move the fabric aside and that snaps him. His hands grip my thighs, pushing them out to reveal my actions to his devouring gaze.

He is the epitome of focus, observing and learning with single-minded concentration. I've never done anything like this. It's the most intimate, vulnerable position I can imagine, but with Beast I'm not uncomfortable or embarrassed. I'm safe in his careful hands. Which makes all of it doubly thrilling and arousing, especially knowing he's never done this with anyone else—or anything close either.

He gets closer, his breath caressing my thigh, his face inches from where my hand circles and plays. Watching him enjoy me in this way is so erotic I nearly come.

He leans in, patience wearing thin, and his tongue flicks against me, brushing my fingers and the flesh between. He presses his tongue against me, following the same pattern. And that does it. I'm shuddering into his mouth and he's tasting me like he could devour me whole.

I ride out the orgasm, his mouth still on me until sensitivity peaks. "Beast." I shove at his shoulder with a half laugh, half strangled groan. "It's too much."

He leans back, still breathing heavy, his eyes opaque with arousal.

"Let me take care of you, too." Sitting up on the seat, I slide next to him, tugging his jeans open before reaching into his pants, gripping his hard length.

Ideas, images flash through my head of all the things I

could do with him. Do to him. Ply him with my hands. My mouth. Both? I pull him out and stroke him up and down, gripping his shaft, marveling at his size—which really is proportional to the rest of him.

A few hard strokes later he's convulsing—shuddering silently, gripping me against him, so strong, but even now while he's out of control, he's careful not to crush me. I feel that restraint down inside my soul.

The moment his body relaxes, a small smile appears.

Wow, he signs.

I lean in and kiss his full lips, wanting to take the sheepish look out of his eyes.

"I could kiss you forever." The words leave my mouth without thought and then I'm mentally cringing. He's going to think I'm a lunatic. In love with him. Desperate and out of my mind.

Well, aren't you? Delores Umbridge asks.

If not, it won't be long.

But he doesn't seem freaked out by my declaration. If anything, his responding ghost of a smile is pleased.

We spend more time kissing, until my mouth is swollen and we have to clean up and get back to the ranch before the sun starts to rise.

We part at the stairs. I stand on the third step up, from a height where we can kiss without him having to bend over. "I wish we could stay the night together," I say against his lips.

He nods, his hands clenching my waist once. I race up the steps to bed, not looking back, otherwise I might not want to leave.

I am in so much trouble.

Chapter Nineteen

HE'S famous for his long—sword.
—Cyrano de Bergerac

The next week passes in a flurry of work and heated moments: shifts at Bodean's, chores for Granny, Beast's wandering hands, more rejections from New York, Beast stealing scorching kisses at work, or in Granny's hallway, or in the barn while everyone else is cleaning up after supper. We barely have any time alone. We can't get any peace at Granny's, not with her and Grace under the same roof, and if we go to Jude's, although the party scene has calmed, there are still people coming and going all the time, even with school out of session.

We haven't told anyone we're together, other than Granny, but we haven't kept it a secret either. Although there is a lingering worry about Grace's potential reaction, which is enough for both of us to keep it relatively quiet and between ourselves.

I don't mind. I kind of like it that Beast waits until no one is looking before he brushes back my hair when we're target shooting out on the back lawn. Or during dinner, when I touch his leg or hold his hand under the table. It's like a secret world between us and no one else knows the language.

By all appearances, Grace is none the wiser, but the others, not so much.

One night, Jude and I run into the house to grab the fixings for s'mores. We've finished Sunday supper and chores and decided to have an impromptu bonfire in the firepit out back.

We're about to head outside, arms laden with chocolate bars, marshmallows, and graham crackers, when Jude stops.

"Fred." His lips are quirked up, but his eyes are serious. "Beast is a big man. His heart is twice the size of us mere mortals'. Be careful with it."

The corresponding organ in my chest twists. I swallow. "The last thing I ever want to do is hurt him."

Jude watches me carefully and then nods once.

Back at the bonfire, we hand out goodies. Grace and Reese scoured the trees for enough sticks for everyone, and before long we all have marshmallows toasting over the flickering flames. The conversation turns to an upcoming trip.

"You won't stay away long, right?" Grace asks Jude.

"It's just a weekend trip, Gracie. Fitz and Annabel haven't seen their parents in months, and I should probably meet them before Annabel's daddy comes after me with his shotgun."

“He wouldn’t do that,” Annabel says. “He has a .357.”

“Beast is staying to look after you and Mr. Bojangles.”

My eyes lock with Beast’s across the fire. There are more than mere physical flames heating the air between us. As if he can read my thoughts, one of his brows quirks up. I tear my gaze away.

“When are you leaving?” I ask.

“Next weekend,” Reese says. “Leaving Friday, won’t be back until Monday. We’ll miss Sunday supper.”

When the next Sunday supper arrives, it is quiet and subdued with only Granny, Grace, Beast, and me. And then Beast has to go home to feed Mr. Bojangles, Jude’s fluffy white cat, and take care of some work for Jude in his absence.

He has to rearrange his schedule to accommodate their needs, and he does it without question. And they just assume he has no other plans or needs of his own. I want to screech at them on his behalf, but I let it go. *None of my business.* Except, isn’t it? If for no other reason than that I want to spend time with Beast, and they’re impinging on it. No, no, *let it go.*

Later that night, I’m on the roof staring up at the stars, alone. Granny fell asleep on the couch downstairs watching *American Horror Story*. I got her sucked into it. She loved the season with the witches, thought it was a hoot, and has been binge-watching it since at every opportunity.

Grace is in her room, where she will likely stay for the rest of the night, and I’m thinking about Beast. In town. At his place. Alone.

Alone.

The word becomes a drum beat pulsing inside me.

This might be our only chance to actually be alone until . . . until for-ev-errrr. Okay, slightly dramatic, but still. I can feel time slipping away, as inexorable as the tide. Within another month—sooner maybe—I'll have enough savings to move back to NYC and find a place to live while continuing to search for work.

But there's no way I can get to Beast's place tonight. I can't take Granny's car. They would hear me leave. They can't know I'm gone. Grace would freak and Granny would probably shoot me. It's at least ten miles, which would take forever to walk.

But there is one other option.

An hour later, I've parked the old beach cruiser on the side of Jude's house. I cleaned it up and helped Granny put on new tires the other week. I'll get it back in the morning before anyone can miss it. Grace doesn't know it exists yet, so no risk of anger from the teen queen.

I knock at the front door and a few moments later, it swings open.

"Hi."

He's staring, motionless. My heart beats faster. The lack of expression kickstarts my urge to ramble.

"Sorry to barge in on you like this. It's just I wanted to see—"

In one quick slice of movement, his hands cup my face and his lips are against mine.

I manage to squeak out words between kisses. "Oh, good." His mouth presses against the corner of my jaw. "I was worried you would think me," he nips at my ear, eliciting a gasp that doesn't stop the flow of words, "weird, desperate," a lick at my neck, "wanton. But I needed to see you."

He shuts the door and locks it, his eyes on me. He slides his arms down to my waist. His big, strong hands hoist me up against him like I weigh less than Mr. Bojangles. My legs lock around his waist and he presses me back against the wall. His mouth is on me, melting me from the inside out. I'm about to turn into a puddle of Fred when he pulls away and turns his head to look down at the floor.

Mr. Bojangles is weaving around Beast's legs, purring up a storm.

I stifle a laugh. "Bad kitty."

Beast kisses my smile and then steps away from the wall, walking down the hallway toward his room without ever putting me down. Mr. Bojangles prances after us, but Beast slips into his room and shuts him out.

Next thing I know, a soft mattress is under my back, and Beast is towering over me, holding himself up so he doesn't crush me, eyes heavy lidded.

I'm ready to start peeling off clothes and riding this stallion. I push my hips up against his, needier than Mr. Bojangles, rubbing myself against his hard length.

He pulls away, far enough to take my face in his hands, eyes searching mine. Then he traces over my features, gazing at me with clear devotion. It's everything. He's loving me with his eyes in a way Jack never did. Like I'm a treasure. A prize. Like I'm the *Firefly* Legacy Edition, signed by Joss Whedon.

This kind of care requires no words. And it's more effective than anything anyone could ever say with mere words.

"Beast," his name is a whisper of need on my lips, "I want you."

He points at himself, then me. *Me, too.*

I press into him, sliding my tongue into his mouth, absorbing the sensations, memorizing everything to lock it away for safekeeping.

He pulls back to sign, *Scared.*

"Of what?"

His smile is small but definitely uneasy. *Too fast.*

"We're moving too fast?" I ask, but he immediately shakes his head no. "Oh, you're worried you'll be too fast."

Already was. Ducks his head to kiss me, hiding the embarrassment.

"It's okay. We have all night and actually, I think it's pretty hot." I swallow, "Knowing that I can make you feel that much. That turned on. Because I am right there with you. You're not alone."

He signs again and my brain is a fuzzy haze of need and want and desire and I have to focus to figure out what he's trying to tell me. *I want to taste you.*

"You want to taste me?" My stomach flips.

He nods.

"I may have just came from you asking."

He grins. *Now?* he spells out.

"Um, yes."

His fingers trip along the waistband of my shorts, rubbing soothing little circles along the delicate skin of my abdomen.

His lips move from my mouth down my neck, fingers plucking at my top. He leans back so I can whip it off over my head and throw it somewhere. His eyes are locked on my chest.

I'm wearing the simplest of bras. It's white, for god's sake. I look like a teenager. On top of that, my chest isn't the best or the biggest. Beast's hands are so large I'm nowhere near a handful, but he's staring at my chest like it's the Ring of Sauron. I guess size is irrelevant.

He traces his fingers around the globes, circling with careful fingers until he's almost at the tips and I'm more than ready for the final contact. But then he pulls away.

I groan. "Beast."

With a wicked grin he leans down and sucks one nipple into his mouth through the cotton. I arch back, my hands going to his hair, threading through the strands. One big hand spreads across my stomach, holding me in place while he uses his other hand to tug the cup of the bra down. His mouth covers me, the heat of it hot and demanding. He lavishes attention on first one and then the other and then he pulls back again, his breath hot and heavy.

Desire is a living, wild thing inside me. Beast kisses down my stomach, tugging at my shorts, pulling them down and off along with my panties until I'm completely bare.

There's no room for embarrassment or worry. His hands are worshipful, rubbing soothing lines up and down my thighs, his eyes hungry. He presses my legs apart with careful strokes while he gazes down at me in wonder.

He leans in, tugging my legs over his broad shoulders, one and then the other, his breath feathering over my heated flesh. My body is as taut as a bowstring stretched tight and waiting for release.

It's relief and torture when he finally kisses me. At first, it's just a careful press of his mouth. Rubbing his lips up and down in soft, sweeping motions. And slowly, the pressure increases.

He's using everything I've shown him, from the first kiss so many weeks ago to the other night when I bared myself to him, guiding his touch. When his tongue finally comes into play, he presses it in slow circles, just like I used my fingers, stroking me with deliberate effort.

When I groan and arch underneath him, I've become a feral creature, holding his head in my hands because I'm about to burst. I roll my hips back and forth, undulating against him, concerned only with my own satisfaction. Only then does his tight control shatter. His tongue thrusts inside and my spine bows with the force of the orgasm ripping through me.

He doesn't let go, instead staying close and gentling his movements as I ride the waves of pleasure until I'm boneless and shaking in the aftermath.

He rests his head on my thigh and looks up at me, his eyes churning with his own leashed desire. Then he stretches up, covering me with his body, braced on his elbows. I'm surrounded in the best of ways.

"You're still wearing clothes," I complain, running hands up his shirt-covered back, lifting it enough to play at the skin just above his belt.

He nuzzles my neck in response.

"It's my turn." I shove at him playfully.

His breath stutters against my skin, a physical manifestation of everything he's holding back. He moves away, kneeling on the bed next to me.

I sit up and cross my arms over my chest in a fake pout. "Time to join the naked party, buddy."

His smile is slow and his eyes dip to my breasts before returning to my face with a lopsided grin.

I tug at his shirt, pulling it over his head. Reaching back, I unsnap my bra and slide it down my shoulders. Beast's eyes are on me, tracking the movements with no attempt to hide the heat in his eager gaze. I push at his big shoulder. He lies back on the bed without resistance, his breath coming out in ragged gasps.

He stills. Watching. Waiting. The bulge in his pants twitches and I tug at the buttons. He helps me undress him until he's as naked as I am.

"That's better." I take him into my hand.

He hisses a breath between his teeth. His hands clench into fists at his side. His head falls back, but he doesn't close his eyes, watching me from beneath lowered lids.

Bending over, I take him into my mouth and revel in the way his body twitches and strains, thighs rigid, stomach muscles bunching and tensing.

I lift up to say, "It's okay to touch me." I grab his hand and put it on my head. His fingers tunnel into my hair.

I lick him like an ice cream cone and then suck on the tip before moving down as much as I can.

His hand flexes against my scalp, the air filled with his rough breathing and the wet sounds of my mouth. Having this giant of man at my mercy floods me with heat and melts everything inside me, a wave that's empowering and arousing. Within minutes, he explodes, shuddering and shaking until his whole body relaxes back on the bed, eyes shut. A gentle hand tugs on my hair, his other pressing at my shoulder, encouraging me to move up from my position between his legs.

Complying, I snuggle up next to him and he wraps an arm around me, pulling me into him and kissing me on the mouth.

He leans back. *Embarrassed.*

“Dude. Any longer and you might have broken my jaw.”

He shakes his head, rolling his eyes at my exaggeration.

“We’ll build it up. It’s not a big deal if you last longer. It’s not like I take forever. In the meantime,” I grin, “this is fun. There’s nothing to be ashamed of here. I like that I turn you on that much. Because you turn me on the same.”

To illustrate the point, I run my hands down his chest, spreading them around his hips, grabbing his butt.

He laughs silently. We spend long minutes enjoying the feel of skin pressed together, reveling in the intimacy of learning each other’s dips and valleys and freckles and scars.

At some point, I must doze off because I’m jarred awake by a pan clanging in the kitchen.

I sit up, glancing around the empty room. I grab one of Beast’s shirts from a drawer. It smells fresh and clean and it goes down past my knees.

Padding down the hall, I stop in the doorway of the kitchen. Beast stands at the stove, putting together a midnight snack. Mr. Bojangles flicks a tail at me, then chases after some invisible foe in the hallway.

Something sizzles on the skillet in front of him. His sweats are slung low on his hips, his back a perfect sculpture of muscles and sinew. I'm getting horny again just watching him.

And he's all mine to do whatever I want with.

For now, Delores Umbridge sneers. I eject her from my brain with a good old-fashioned *expelliarmus*. This night is not meant for thoughts of tomorrow. If this is all I get, I intend to enjoy every second.

Chapter Twenty

"WELL I GUESS if I had to choose . . . I'd marry Swamp Thing, screw the Hulk, and still kill Aquaman."

–Overheard at Comic-Con

Beast must sense my simmering perusal because he turns, eyes sliding to my toes and back up, a motion as effective as a caress. His eyes are bright and his mouth tips up at the corners.

He holds out his arm and I immediately move into his side. With his free hand, he flips the sandwich frying in the pan, exposing a perfectly toasted, golden surface.

"Grilled cheese." I point at the other simmering pot. "And tomato soup? Smells delicious." On the counter, he's spread a variety of cheeses and artisan bread. Of course. I'd bet money the soup is homemade. He releases me after a quick squeeze and moves away to grab something from the fridge. I pick up a nearby spoon and stir the soup.

A few seconds later, he's behind me, not touching, but

his broad expanse emits enough heat to span my entire back.

His fingers play at the hem of his stolen shirt, knuckles brushing against the backs of my thighs.

Air hisses between his teeth the moment he realizes I've got nothing on underneath. He's motionless behind me, not moving, just breathing. I help him out a little, tugging the shirt up and exposing my bottom to the air.

He moves, fingers tracing my skin, nuzzling at the back of my neck, lips sucking and nipping at the corner where my neck meets my shoulder. I gasp and arch into him.

"Beast. Touch me."

That's all the encouragement he needs. His fingers slide between my legs from behind. I'm turned on already, his fingers slipping against me with ease.

There's a humming rumble in his chest, reverberating through my back and into my whole body. I press against him, his hard length a rod against my spine. His breath whooshes in my ear. His fingers play me like an instrument, one hand sliding up under the shirt to pluck at my nipples while his other explores between my legs.

Within minutes I'm shuddering against him, hands up behind me and locked around his neck while he tortures me into sweet oblivion.

When I finally come back down to earth, I turn into him. My arms circle around his waist, holding on but boneless. One of his hands strokes my back while the other cups my bottom.

I speak into his chest. "I didn't know I could orgasm so many times in a twenty-four-hour period."

I lean back to catch his expression. It's a new smile, not like his lopsided grin or sheepish tipped corner, this smile is wide and satisfied, all male satisfaction. His cock is a hard, needy length between us.

"It's my turn."

His brows lift.

"Feel free to keep cooking so it doesn't burn." I glance behind me at the food. "I'm starving. But I think I'll go for an appetizer."

I kneel in front of him.

He lets out a big breath and before I can pull down his shorts, he reaches down, scooping me into his arms bridal style.

"What about the food?"

His eyes flick from me to the food, in the direction of the bedroom and then back to me.

"I'm hungry, big man. And we need energy if we're going to keep this up."

His eyes brighten further, one brow quirking.

"You're going to be insatiable, aren't you?"

He nods.

"I can't say I have a problem with it."

Walking quickly, he carries me to his room and literally tosses me on the bed. Then he holds up a finger and disappears for a few minutes, coming back with a tray laden with food.

"Food and Beast. It really doesn't get any better than this."

We eat and fool around and spend time exploring, experimenting, teaching the other how to best bring pleasure. Learning things about him and myself that I didn't know before. Then we snuggle, entwined like vines. My favorite position is lying on his chest, listening to the slow and steady beat of his heart while caressing the ridges of his body.

His lamp is on, sitting on his desk in the corner. It's a muted light, a soft glow adding to the quiet comfort. Our own little world.

"George. Does anyone else know your real name? I mean, besides Jude and Grace."

He shakes his head.

"Did you sign up for school using your real name?"

He smiles. Shakes his head again.

"Why do you go by Beast and not George?"

He takes a breath, watching me, and then comes to some sort of internal decision. He starts to sign more, but then holds up a finger and grabs his phone from the bedside table.

It's a nickname Jude gave me. We met him at the library in Valdosta. Grace would use the computers and Jude was there a lot, too. He said I would glower so hard, he could hear it. Like I was growling. It became a bit of a joke. My real name has bad memories so it stuck.

I pat his chest. "Beast definitely fits. But you also registered under Beast. How the heck did you pull that off?"

Jude signed me up for school when we came here looking for Grace.

I tilt my head. "Annabel mentioned something about Grace running away and coming here. It must have been terrible for you. I bet you were so worried."

He nods.

"You have been through a lot together."

He nods again. *I'm glad we're here. Having a stable home, and Granny, helped mellow Grace out a lot.*

I turn, scooting to face him more fully. "Why does your real name have bad memories?"

He's unmoving for long enough that I'm not sure he's going to answer. But there's no tension in him, he's relaxed as he rubs a hand up and down my arm. Then he starts typing.

Grace is my half sister. Same mother, different dads. My dad died when I was little.

"Beast. I'm sorry." My arms tighten reflexively around him, as if I can reach inside to the boy he was.

He presses a kiss to the top of my head and keeps typing. *A few years later, Mom started dating Grace's dad and they had Grace. Grace's dad took off when Mom was pregnant. I don't even know if he knows she exists. Our mom had some problems with drugs.*

I almost ask him to stop, wanting to shield him from his own past, but he keeps going.

Mom wasn't always, he stops for a second, head turning to the wall, thinking, *present. Even if she was physically there, she always seemed unaware, of me or anything else. I learned how to find my own food because she would often forget to eat herself. I had issues with stuttering. Mom got better when she was pregnant with Grace. Less volatile, more aware. But then after Grace was born, things got bad again. Eventually, we were taken from her and sent to live with our uncle, Mom's brother.*

He lifts his hand to rub his chin.

"It's okay if you don't want to tell me everything. I know it must be hard." Even this, the least of details, is hard to envision. I can't imagine what an upbringing like that would do to a child, let alone this sweet giant of a man who even now rubs a hand over my back, soothing me, when he's the one sharing his difficult past.

He shakes his head and returns to thumbing over the phone.

It was fine at first. Our uncle wasn't a bad guy. He was a mechanic. But then he hurt his back and was laid off. And then everything changed. He changed.

I don't think he minded raising us at first. But after he lost his job, money got tight. I needed new shoes every month. Grace liked to take things apart to see how they worked, the toaster, clocks, computers, the microwave. He couldn't afford to replace things and we were too young to understand. We were a lot to deal with. And he hadn't wanted kids. We weren't his. I think he resented us. I know at some point he started dealing drugs to get money. Things sort of got better for a time. Then they got worse when he started using.

He puts the phone down, his hand running down my back and pulling me tighter against him, like he needs to remember where he is and it's not back there. He's not a child dependent on adults he can never trust, with a sister he's trying to defend.

"How old were you during all this?"

Nine when Mom died. Grace was four. When we left our uncle, I was thirteen and Grace was eight.

That makes sense since Grace is fourteen and Beast is nineteen. They've only been in Blue Falls for a little over a year, which means it's been them against the world for five years.

When he started using and things got real bad, I was maybe ten or eleven. He used to yell at us a lot to shut up while he was doing his deals or having parties in the garage. It was important we keep quiet, stay away, not catch the attention of his friends. In some ways, I think it was to protect us. If we misbehaved, he would withhold food, even water sometimes. Stopped letting us go to school. I used to sneak into neighbors' houses to get food for us.

My chest constricts at the thought of Grace and Beast as children, forced into taking care of their most basic needs at a time when they should have had no worries beyond school and making friends.

It was hard for Grace. She was curious about everything, a chatterbox. I was never a big talker because of the stuttering. But I had to take care of Grace. I tried to turn it into a game, who could go the longest without talking. Once during one of his parties we were watching a movie in our room and when I went to use the bathroom, she snuck out. I had to go after her, get her back before anyone saw. But I got caught. He locked me in a closet for three days as punishment.

My body tenses and flashes with cold. "Beast." My voice is thick with emotion. "You don't have to keep going."

But he just shakes his head and continues.

After that he told me, if I messed up again, he would do the same to Grace, or worse. That's when the anxiety was nearly uncontrollable. I had even more trouble speaking. Even when he wasn't around, I would remember what he said and my throat would fill to the point I couldn't talk around it. And then I went so long without talking, at some point it was too late to go back.

A tear slips out of my eye and lands on his chest. "I'm so sorry. Is your uncle dead? Tell me he's dead. If he's not, can we kill him?"

He shakes his head, his hand rubbing my arm. Consoling me.

He went to prison a few years after we left. I knew I had to be stronger, so I started doing whatever I could, running, push-ups. I was growing like crazy at the time. By the time I turned thirteen I was over six feet tall. We made a plan and left. You know Grace is smart. We took care of each other. She got us money using computers. And then we found Jude. Or he found us.

"You found each other." I sit up and face him, climbing on top of him to cup his giant face in my palms, his stubble scratching my palms. "Thank you for sharing your past with me."

His hands move between us.

Not scared yet? he signs.

I shake my head. "You saved Grace, and you saved yourself. You are not defined by your trauma. You are defined by your resilience. You are the best person I know."

His arms go around me, crushing me to his chest, and I hang on tight. After a while, he grabs his phone again, holding it in front of me to read.

You are not the sum of your experiences either.

"I hardly think my shitty breakup can compare to what you've been through in your life."

He's motionless for a spell, and I know him well enough to know he's considering his words. *You care about people, too. You aren't the sidekick, you're the main character.*

I laugh. "You're saying I need to be the hero in my own story."

You already are.

"Thank you. I had already kinda figured that out, but I like the way you put it better. You have a way with words."

And then he smiles. A heartbreaking, happy grin that crinkles his eyes.

My breath catches in my throat.

I'm pretty sure my heart is gone. Toast. Donezo. And despite the inevitable pain looming on the horizon, loving him will be the most exquisite self-destructive decision I've made yet.

Chapter Twenty-One

"ARE you trying to bring the fandom here?"

"I am the fandom."

–Overheard at Comic-Con

It's still early when I wake up, wrapped in a cocoon of warmth and sweet-smelling man. Beast is sprawled across the bed and I'm lying half on top of him. There's no choice in the matter, considering he takes up the entire mattress.

But I'm not uncomfortable. I could stay here forever.

He makes me want to give it all up. Maybe I could work remotely. Or I could really be a homeless wretch and hang out in front of the H-E-B with Ol' Roy.

My phone emits a muffled chirrup. My purse is out in the entry where I dropped it last night.

I wiggle out of bed and race to answer it. It might be Granny. She's probably realized I'm gone and now she's totally freaking.

I pick up my phone and it's a New York area code.

Frowning, I answer. "Hello?"

"Fredericka? It's Amber. From Comix."

"Oh." Surprise colors my voice. "Hi Amber, I'm surprised to hear from you."

I squint at the clock in the kitchen. It's early yet. Six thirty. But that would make it eight thirty in New York.

"I bet. Listen, I'm really sorry about the email that was sent."

This is weird. A former prospective employer calling to apologize about their rejection of me?

She continues, the sound of traffic and wind muffling her voice, like she's walking the streets of the city. Something in my heart lurches at the sound. I didn't realize I missed it until now. "Apparently there was some kind of glitch in our system and it sent you the standard refusal notice. It shouldn't have mattered, because I've been trying to call you for the past week anyway to offer you a position, but each time I tried to call you from the office, it would ring to a Domino's. IT said somehow the calls were being routed wrong. So I finally decided to try from my personal cell, and it worked!"

"That's . . . so weird."

Grace.

It has to be. And another thought strikes me in that moment. If she did something to sabotage my chances with this job, someone she's only known for a few months, what would she do to keep Beast around?

"So what do you think?"

I snap back into the call.

"About . . ." Does she know I know who messed with their system?

But Amber just laughs. "About the job. Are you interested?"

My whole body tightens. "Yes. Absolutely yes."

"Awesome. I'll email you the details when I get back to the office. Call me on this number if you don't get it, though. We're looking at a start date in two weeks. Does that work for you?"

My limbs loosen again, everything sinking. "Yes. That works."

It will be tight, but I'll make it work.

We hang up and after taking a million deep breaths and pinching myself to make sure I'm not still asleep and dreaming or hallucinating or something, I head back to Beast's room.

I sit on the edge of the bed, trying not to disturb him, but he feels me anyway.

Rolling in my direction, he opens his eyes and greets me with a sleepy grin. His hair is askew, his wide, muscled chest enticing in the early morning sun.

More than anything, I want to cuddle into him and forget the world, but I can't.

"I got the job." The words tumble out of my mouth.

He sits up on his elbows, blinking at me.

For a brief moment, I wonder if he's going to get upset, but then the grin returns, bigger than before and he pulls me into a bear hug.

He's thrumming with excitement, still smiling when he pulls away to sign, *I'm so proud of you.*

"You are?"

He nods.

"But this means—" My throat closes up and I swallow past the lump forming there. "I have to leave."

His smile droops. He shrugs and grabs his phone. *We knew this was going to happen, right?*

"Right." I swallow and then the word vomit happens. "Come with me."

His brows lift.

"Apply to culinary school. To CIA in New York. You'll get in, I know it. Then you can come with me."

He blinks rapidly, but then shakes his head slowly. *I can't. You know I can't.*

I grip his hand in mine, like the pressure itself will make him change his mind. "But you can. I have to tell you what they said. You know how they sent me an email rejection?"

He nods.

I quickly explain what Amber said about the calls being routed and the email being an accident.

"It might have been Grace."

He looks away, toward the window before typing into the phone. *It might have been.*

"If it was, don't you see? She might have done the same thing to you when you applied before."

He stares at me for a few long seconds, expression inscrutable. But then he just shakes his head again. *Even if she did, it doesn't matter. I can't move away.*

"Grace and Jude love you. They should want what's best for you, too, and what if that isn't here?"

What if they are his Jack? Whether they realize it or not.

Grace needs me. She puts on a front, but she's not like other kids her age. Her childhood was not normal. She needs constancy and I'm the only one who's been there since the beginning. I'm the only one who knows, who really understands.

Hot tears threaten. I know it's a lot to ask, for him to leave his only family, the only people he's loved to be with me, but I want to be the one that comes first for him. It's unfair and selfish. Grace is only fourteen, she needs him more than I do, and I can't stay. Not even this burgeoning romance, epic as it might feel, can stop me from following my dreams. Even if it means breaking my own heart. I can't have another Jack in my life, but I also can't be the Jack in his.

A dull ache thumps behind my eyes, and I press my fingers to my temples like it will keep the pain at bay.

So what if Grace and Jude are the Jacks? Maybe everyone is someone else's Jack. Maybe it doesn't matter. Maybe life isn't always neat and tidy and people don't fit into the boxes we want to place them in. Maybe it won't be perfect, but maybe that's okay. Isn't it?

"If you could move, would you? If Grace didn't need you, or if she was . . . older?"

He nods, his eyes both wistful and sad. *If there were any other way, I would go with you in a heartbeat. This is Grace's first chance for something normal and stable, finally, and I can't take it from her. Maybe someday, when she's older, but not now.*

I nod. "I know. I get it." I brush away the wet streaking down my face with the back of my hand.

He crushes me to him. Kisses my tears away. His chest vibrates under my cheek. He's trying to speak but can't. Only a moan emerges.

He pushes me away and snatches his phone. For the first time, he's visibly frustrated with his lack of speech and my heart twists.

He types into the phone, but it takes a little longer than usual. *We can make this work. Just because you are following your dreams doesn't mean you can't be a part of mine.*

I put my hand on the side of his face, rubbing a thumb over his cheek. Holding the memory of his words inside me. I'm a part of his dreams. Nothing has ever felt so good or right. But . . . "How? How is it going to work if I'm two thousand miles away?" The question is a desperate plea, and he meets it with a firm jaw and another question.

Do you want this to work?

"Yes. Of course."

Then it will. There is no one else for me. The look he tosses me after I read his words is a challenge.

I stiffen my spine. "Me, too."

Good, he mouths, then he chucks the phone to the side and tugs me into him.

Later that afternoon, we're back at the ranch. Grace is on the couch, Jude and Beast on either side of her, and Granny and I sit across from them.

I wasn't sure that I should be present at all, but Granny insisted that I be there since Grace's actions have directly affected me and she wants Grace to have to deal with the consequences.

Earlier today, the happy couples returned from visiting

Annabel and Fitz's parents. Beast and I told Jude the story, and he was able to confirm Grace's virtual shenanigans using technology and know-how that is beyond my capabilities. I was right. She messed with Comix's phone and email systems.

Too much time has passed for Jude to confirm if she also messed with Beast's past culinary school application, but it doesn't seem to matter much to him anyway.

When confronted, at first Grace denies having anything to do with the phony email and call routing, but when Jude shows her how he was able to track it back to her, she bursts into tears, burying her face in Beast's shoulder.

"I'm sorry," she tells me when the first round of tears has abated.

"I forgive you." How could I not?

Granny rolls her eyes at my easy acquiescence. "It's not right to mess with people's lives. This is someone you care about."

"I know. It's just . . . Fred, I don't want you to leave." She's leaning into Beast, Jude holding one of her hands on the other side. I reach out and take her free hand.

"I'm not dying. We'll still be friends. And I've told you, you can come stay with me anytime."

"People come and go in your life, baby girl," Jude says with a squeeze of her hand. "And Fred won't be one of them. I reckon she's gonna stick whether she lives here or not." He winks at me.

Grace looks at me and then Beast and back again. "I don't want you to leave Beast either. I know you've been together and trying to hide it from me. You can't hurt him."

Beast and I lock eyes for a second and I pat Grace's hand. "What's happening between Beast and me is between us. But I would never hurt him. I couldn't."

It would be like stabbing myself in the heart, but I can't admit that much in front of everyone.

She nods and looks up at him.

He signs something to her, and I don't catch all of it with my limited knowledge, but he promises her something.

"I know," Grace says. "I promised never to leave you again either, and I'm sticking to it."

I squeeze her hand and let go. Even though I know it's the only way things can be, any lingering hope I might have had that Beast would come to New York with me shatters and my heart pinches tight at the unfairness of it all.

"It . . . it sucks getting close to people because then you get hurt," Grace mutters.

Granny reaches out and puts her hands over Grace's knee. "My darling. Life without connection is no life at all. And since we're here now, and being honest, there's something I've been meaning to bring up." She sits back and clears her throat, her hands clasping in her lap.

I exchange another glance with Beast. Granny is never nervous. Stubborn, eccentric, annoyed, impatient, yes. She definitely runs the gamut of moods. But never this.

"You should all know." She pauses for a long moment and panic twists in my stomach. What if she's sick or something? "I've been seeing someone."

We stare at her.

Grace is the first to speak. "Seeing . . . someone?"

"Romantically," she confirms.

"Why Granny, you're breaking my heart," Jude deadpans, the perfect response to make everyone, including Granny, chuckle.

She swipes at him. "You're a rascal, Jude boy, and that's what I love about you."

"This is why you've been sneaking out all the time?" Grace asks. "Why didn't you tell me?"

"Now, Gracie, don't get upset. I wasn't hiding it from you because you don't matter, I was hiding it because you do. I don't want to bring anyone into your life that isn't going to stick around long-term. If it ended up just being a quick flirtation, there was no reason to get too attached. You understand."

Grace's eyes are wide, still reddened from her earlier upset. "So you're saying it's serious now?"

"It is. And I want to invite her over for supper so y'all can meet her, if that's okay."

My brows lift. "Her?"

Granny squints at me. "That's what I said."

I lift both hands in surrender. "I, for one, would love to meet her. Who is she?"

"Elaine Kilgariff."

Jude grins. "That lady you're always trying to get the fried chicken recipe from?"

Granny nods. "We've been friends for a long time, but things have escalated. That's all I'm sayin' about it now, ya hear?"

I wrap an arm around Granny's shoulder. "I think it's wonderful."

"Me, too," Grace says.

Beast nods.

Grace clears her throat and then bites her lip, her gaze darting around us. "Since we're doing this whole sharing thing, I should probably mention I lied about the kids being mean to me at school. I didn't want friends because I didn't think we'd stay here this long."

"Oh, Grace," I say.

"This one guy tried to sit with me at lunch and I might have barked at him."

I can't hold back my laugh, and Grace gives me a watery smile. "I just figured, if they think I'm crazy, they'll leave me alone."

Jude shifts on the couch, turning to face her. "Why would you want to be alone when you and I both know how desperately you want friends?"

"It's too scary. Computers I can understand. I can control them. But people do whatever they want and it doesn't make sense."

"Amen, sister."

Granny smacks my shoulder. "Don't encourage her."

My eyes lock with Beast and for a tangled second, I completely understand why Grace would go out of her way to avoid getting closer to people. I've barely had any time at all with Beast in the grand scheme of things, but my heart . . . it already hurts.

Chapter Twenty-Two

I MAY CLIMB PERHAPS to no great heights, but I will climb alone.

–Cyrano de Bergerac

Two weeks fly by at warp speed.

My parents are ecstatic. Even though they still don't really understand the concept of the work I'll be doing, they're happy I found something I enjoy that isn't bearded lady at a circus.

Scarlett has offered an escape if staying with my parents becomes intolerable. She and Guy live in a palatial apartment on the Upper East Side. But they also live with Guy's teen sisters—twins—and Scarlett only moved in with him recently. Talk about intruding. I should have started apartment hunting already, but I've been slammed with making preparations to move myself and my meager belongings across the country, finishing out my last two weeks at Bodean's, and spending every spare minute with Beast.

I've been memorizing our moments. His smell, his taste, the feel of his scruffy jaw under my fingers. Each sensation is amplified a thousandfold knowing our time is numbered.

Despite the bonding, apologetic conversation with Grace, she's been avoiding me and when she's forced into my presence, she barely talks. She doesn't even fight me for the bathroom in the mornings.

All of this makes my last shift at Bodean's a muddle.

"Hey, Lucas." I grab an apron from the cupboard.

"Wait."

I freeze, apron in hand and turn.

"Before you put that on, Ranger wanted to talk to you up front."

I grimace. "This isn't going to be an awkward goodbye thing, right?"

He chuckles. "I'm sure it's nothing of the sort."

I push open the swinging doors to enter the bar area. It's dark. "Is there a problem with the power?" I call back to Lucas.

The lights blink on and— "Surprise!"

Mouth agape, I just stare at the small group clustered in the center of the room, whooping and laughing at my no doubt ridiculous face.

Lucas comes out of the kitchen behind me carrying a sheet cake with the words *Congratulations Fred!* Scrawled in bright blue and red frosting.

So naturally, I burst into tears.

I'm immediately surrounded by people, Granny

patting me on the back. "It's your party and you cry if you need to."

Eliza smacks me on the shoulder. "Pull yourself together, woman. You have to see the food Beast made. You didn't tell me your man was a chef."

Reese is on my other side, giving me a sideways hug. "We were going to invite more people, but Beast said you don't like big crowds."

"Thank you," I tell her sincerely, wiping at my eyes.

"I totally get it."

They draw me over to a table festooned with ribbons and decorated with superhero paraphernalia. Lucas sets down the sheet cake and I get a closer look. The *o*'s in congratulations are Spider-Man and Black Panther faces.

The rest of the spread follows the same theme: Batman bun sandwiches, a fruit tray of strawberries, bananas, and blueberries arranged to make Captain America's shield, and Wonder Woman lasso fries.

I lift my gaze and lock eyes on Beast.

A thousand thoughts and feelings flash between us, words rendered unnecessary. I walk around the table and reach up. He meets me halfway, kissing me senseless in front of everyone. Whoops and hollers surround us, but it doesn't matter.

I pull away to look into his face, his arms still around my waist. "Thank you."

One more quick kiss and then Annabel yanks me away to the dance floor where Jude has set up two Doctor Who–style telephone booths. He explains the challenge—to see who can change into a superhero costume the fastest—and I laugh.

Grace is already inside of one of them pushing buttons and messing with the door, sliding it open and closed.

Granny brought her girlfriend, Elaine, who we all met at supper last weekend. They're very formal with each other in front of us, but also sweet when they don't think we're watching. Elaine makes sure Granny gets an extra-large slice of cake after we eat.

We spend a couple of hours playing games, laughing and talking. Granny wins the superhero challenge. Ranger teases Annabel and Jude about some night when he caught them making out in his office, a story they refuse to elaborate on. Lucas talks to Beast about recipes, and Eliza informs me that when I leave, Beast will be moving from security into the kitchen. Ranger and Eliza also take great delight in teasing me and telling everyone how I manhandle the bar accoutrements and clean like I'm trying to murder all the dirt.

I very vehemently blame Caroline for all of the ill treatment, much to Beast's delight.

Later, I get a moment to talk with Jude while the others are distracted. Despite a little voice in my head telling me to *let it go*, this time, I just can't. "Remember how you told me to take care of Beast's heart?"

He nods, his gaze curious.

"You should take care of it, too. Make sure when you ask him for help with things that it's not the morning after a late shift. And that he's taking time to do what he wants, instead of what makes the rest of you happy."

His brows lift, mouth popping open. But then he huffs out a breath, pressing his lips together and grimacing. "I suppose you're right. We do tend to take advantage of his helpful nature and he wouldn't be the type to deny assistance to anyone." He tilts his head. "I can see you have his best interests at heart."

I smile, though I'm sure it looks a little wilted. "Thank you for listening and not getting defensive."

"When you love someone, it's not about being right. It's about doing what's right. We are none of us perfect." He nudges his shoulder against mine. "And that's all right."

Afterward, Beast drives us back to his house. We're alone, the others staying behind to help with cleanup.

We walk into the house hand in hand.

"Thank you," I tell him once we're in his room together. "Most of the time, even for my birthday, my parents just take me to dinner or whatever. No one has ever done anything like this for me."

He mouths and signs at the same time to make sure I understand, *You're worth it.*

I reach up and grab his face. He leans into me and then we're kissing. The gentle press of mouths and the slide of tongues are familiar and comforting, but also tinged with a thread of desperation.

This is it.

Our last night. He's driving me to the airport tomorrow afternoon and then . . . who knows when I'll be able to kiss him again?

I shove the thoughts away and focus on taking off his clothes. I want nothing more than the press of his skin against mine, his warmth surrounding me. I want to crawl inside him. His lips trail from my mouth to my jaw and down the length of my neck.

"Beast."

He moves back and looks at me.

"I want you." I search his face to make sure he understands my meaning. We haven't had sex yet, but I want it with a force that's almost frightening in its intensity.

He nods and mouths, *Yes. I want you, too. So much.*

"Are you sure?"

He smiles. Pulls his phone from his pocket and types, *Worried about my virtue?*

"I am, like, three years older than you. Practically a cougar."

His smile widens. *Consider me corrupted.* I giggle, and this time he signs, *I want only you. Everything. You.*

My laughter dies. I force the word through the lump in my throat. "Yes."

Then his hands are at my clothes, unbuttoning my work blouse, his large fingers trembling as he slides each button out of the small holes.

As soon as my top meets the floor, I'm tugging at his T-shirt. He pulls it over his head and then the rest of our clothes find themselves tangled together around us.

I'm a jumble of sensations. The press of his mouth to mine, the whisper of his hands mapping out my body with the tips of his fingers. I push him down to the bed and then straddle him. The hard length of him pressing my most sensitive spot yanks a gasp of pleasure from me. I am not going to last long, at least not this first time.

"Condom?"

He nods at the bedside table and I lean over to grab it,

sheathing him before our mouths connect again. I sit up, wanting to watch him even as I possess him.

Grabbing his length between us, I position him and then settle myself around his length. I move slowly, taking care, adjusting to his size. He fills me, stretching me in the best of ways until we are fully merged. Once he's all the way in, I maintain our visual connection, not wanting to let go of it even for a second. His eyes gleam, dark as night. His fingers trace up my skin, giant hands clasping around my nape, thumbs brushing my cheeks, holding me with a fierce devotion I feel all the way down to my toes.

For long moments we breathe together, joined in the most intimate of ways.

Then I start moving.

Before long, he's gasping, his hands moving down, clenching my hips. I move with rhythmic slowness, up and down. The pent-up emotion, the love, the loss, it's all there in the rigid line of his body, his taut cheeks, his skin stretched tight over his bones. His features are stark, hardened with passion.

I move faster. His hands smooth up my skin, thrumming at my nipples, then one hand slides between our bodies, rubbing me just how he knows I like it. An orgasm rips through me like a tidal wave, his name on my lips.

He pumps up into me, his hands seizing my hips.

Then he's shuddering, gasping, falling with me and we land back on the earth together.

Chapter Twenty-Three

"THEY REALLY GAVE me a hard time at the airport over my Wakandan passport."

–Overheard at Comic-Com

"You'll never understand how much I'm going to miss you. We've had good times and bad times, but you've come to mean so much to me."

Kylo Hen's shimmering feathers twitch with her jerky neck movements, one golden eye flickering at me before she pecks at my shoes.

"I know, I know. You'll miss me, too, in your own little birdie way. Don't forget about me. Be good for Granny. Try to stay out of the moonshine."

"Fred girl," Granny calls from outside the coop.

"Coming," I yell back.

Granny is waiting for me in the middle of the yard. "Beast is here to drive you to the airport."

We walk up to the house together and we're halfway

there before Granny speaks again. "Grace is hiding somewhere. I'm not sure she'll be out to say goodbye."

I nod, unable to speak through the lump forming in my throat.

"She doesn't deal with people leaving the way most of us do. We're sad, but we know it's not forever. She hasn't quite figured that bit out yet. She doesn't know that just because someone leaves, it doesn't mean they're gone." With that, Granny puts an arm around my shoulders. "Be patient. Stay in touch. She'll come around. It will be good for her.

"Thanks, Granny. I will. And thank you for . . . everything. You saved me at a time when I didn't even know I needed the rescue."

"Oh, Fred girl, don't you know? You saved us, too."

I manage to hold it together while saying goodbye to the others. Jude carries my bag to the truck before giving me a hard, swift hug, followed by Fitz. I only have the one bag, everything else was shipped, and there wasn't much.

Reese and Annabel squish me between them, promising to text and call.

Granny gives me one last hug, squeezing me tight. "Give your momma my regards, and tell Scarlett to bring that handsome man and his family down for a visit."

"I will."

"Good luck with your new job, and remember, the road to hell wasn't paved in a day."

I laugh. "I'll always remember that, Granny."

And then I'm in the truck with Beast, heading down the driveway, then through Blue Falls, down Main Street. Past the Finer Diner. Past the H-E-B, waving to Ol' Roy.

It's both the longest and shortest drive in the whole damn world. I want to get it over with, but at the same time I want it to never end.

Beast parks at the curb, gets my bag out of the back, and opens my door for me. People move around us, dragging their luggage.

I can't meet his eyes. I might lose it. He kisses me with my eyes shut, like that will keep the emotion away. Tears threaten to overwhelm me, especially when the kiss turns into gentle pecks, first my top lip, then the bottom, brushing his nose against mine before pulling away, his hands surrounding the back of my neck.

I keep my eyes shut. "You'll come to visit as soon as you can?"

But of course, he can't answer unless I open my eyes. His thumbs brush my cheeks and I blink my eyes open.

I immediately want to close them again. Beast's eyes are glassy, lined in red.

I can't handle this.

"The very first break in school, we'll see each other. We'll make it happen."

He nods.

"Why does a few months feel like a lifetime?"

He kisses me again, this time harder and swifter.

"Can we have phone sext?"

That generates a smile, a small upturning of his lips, but it doesn't chase the shadows from his eyes.

"I better go." My mouth is dry, my stomach threatening to revolt.

I want to say it. I almost say it.

I love you.

But I can't. It's too hard.

Instead I kiss him, one last time.

"This isn't goodbye. It's see you later."

And on that super lame parting—which fits, considering our history—I grab my bag and walk inside. I don't look back. If I do, I might not be strong enough to leave.

The flight home is a blur. I can't see much through my tears. My mind keeps going back to those final moments with Beast and everything that I'm leaving behind.

Now I understand why Bella was so depressed in *New Moon*. We may as well be Edward and Bella . . . minus the sparkly skin and blood drinking and you know, gross and questionable hundred-year age gap.

My seatmate gives me a wide berth, but things start looking better when I've downed three of those little booze containers.

I manage to pull myself together by the time the plane is taxiing on the runway at JFK.

Exiting the terminal, a group of people clustered near the escalator wave at me. It's my parents, along with Scarlett, Guy, and his two little sisters, Emma and Ava.

They're holding up signs. Scarlett's reads *Welcome Home and Prosper* with the Vulcan hand sign drawn next to it. Dad's makes me laugh out loud: *Fred, I am your father*. There's another one, but Emma swings it toward Ava's head right as I'm trying to read it.

I wave and run toward them, and then I'm surrounded by family and friends.

"I missed all of you," I say between hugs and cheek kisses.

I breathe in my mother's lemony scent. It is good to be home.

This time, when my eyes blur, I can't help but smile, too.

~

Apartment hunting in New York City is like trying to defeat the White Walkers blindfolded with one hand tied behind my back. I spend a few days searching ads and listings before I find something larger than a closet without twenty percent broker fees.

And I don't even find it myself.

My phone rings in the morning, a week after moving back. I'm in my old bedroom, moping around like a scrub, un-showered, unhappy, reveling in misery, but trying nonetheless.

"I emailed you a number and address. Call it and tell them Sophia sent you."

"Hi Grace, it's so nice to hear from you."

She sighs.

"Stop rolling your eyes at me."

"I didn't."

"You always sigh when you're rolling your eyes at me."

She's quiet for a moment. "Fine."

I grab my laptop from where I left it on my nightstand and pull up my email. "So what's this number you want me to call?"

"I found an apartment for you, it's one subway ride to your work, and it's in Manhattan. There are no broker fees, it's rent controlled, and it's a thousand square feet and in your budget."

"Grace . . . you didn't kill someone, did you?"

"No." She laughs and my heart squeezes a little. "I did a little digging. For me, this was nothing. But it's going be snapped up soon. You need to call them today."

"I will. Assuming this isn't some elaborate trick because you want me to come back to Blue Falls and strangle you."

She chuckles. "Don't be a stranger."

"I'll call you every day."

Tapping in the background. She's on her computer, even now. "Not necessary. Email me."

"Why? So you can hack my accounts?"

She groans. "I'd only do things that were nice."

"I know."

She blows out a breath. "I'm sorry. I didn't say goodbye."

"It's okay. I understand. I'm sad, too. It's okay to be sad, but I'll always be your friend. And I'll always be a phone call or plane ride away."

We hang up and I call the number in her email, rattling off the address I'm inquiring about when someone answers.

There's a long pause. "We haven't even listed that property yet."

How did she . . . I remember her other instructions. "Uh, Sophia sent me."

"Oh. Right. Did you want to take a look today?"

"Yes. Please."

Miraculously, the apartment is perfect and because I

have my paperwork and down payment ready—because that's how you do it in New York if you want to get it done—I can move in within the next two weeks.

Later that afternoon, while I'm presenting a well-thought-out argument to my parents on the benefits of eating takeout as opposed to my mother's cooking, I get a text from Beast.

Did you get the apartment?

A heat wave rolls through my body and I race upstairs to get away from my parents' prying gazes.

I got it! Did Grace tell you?

A few long seconds pass before he replies. *She did. She told me about emailing you the details, but I convinced her to call.*

I lie down on my bed, clutching my phone like a lifeline. *You can be very convincing. Thank you. The place is perfect. How are things in BF?*

It's good. Picking up extra shifts at Bodean's to help in the kitchen.

There's another long pause with the text bubble dotting my screen.

I miss you.

I miss you, too. And then before I can chicken out, I tug down my tank top, take a probably not that sexy but topless duck-face selfie, and send the picture.

His response is immediate. *Damn. I think you're trying to kill me.*

I laugh and wish I could see his face, his dark gaze capturing me like a fist.

He's still typing. *You're too gorgeous. Now I want to get on the next flight to New York.*

I wouldn't stop you.

I'm coming to visit as soon as I can.

It's not soon enough.

The very next day, the whirlwind begins. Shopping, working, moving into my new place. Staying busy and occupied is literally the only reason I haven't totally lost my shit.

I've exchanged some texts with the others, not just Beast. It's not the same and my heart aches with the loss, the yearning unbearable if I dwell on it for too long. So I don't. Instead, I keep going.

The job is brilliant. Everyone is awesome and into geeky pop culture. I have to work with a marketing team, which is scary at first, but they actually listen to me like I'm a human being with value and insight.

To celebrate, my parents take me with them to Blossom on Ninth for Thursday night dinner.

It's not Sunday supper at Granny's. There are no "Dearly beloveds," and it's just me and the parents, but I make an attempt to enjoy myself nonetheless.

I text Beast on my way home in the cab but don't get a response. A glance at the clock tells me why. He's working. An ache builds in my chest. I wish I could see his face. I miss him so much.

Tears threaten and I force myself to take a deep breath and avert my attention to unpacking my apartment.

It's almost finished. I didn't have much to begin with. My parents gave me an old hand-me-down sofa and TV set. I brought my old bed from home. I have a small kitchen and dining nook, which opens into the living room, and then there's a small bedroom and connecting bathroom with a claw-foot tub and standing shower. It's practically a mansion by New York standards.

Once I've finished hanging a picture on the wall, my only picture, I step back to admire it. Beast mailed it to me last week to celebrate my new pad. It's a framed quote from Stan Lee. "If you have an idea that you genuinely think is good, don't let some idiot talk you out of it," I read out loud.

I've been avoiding hanging it up, because while I love it, seeing it there every day reminds me of what I'm missing.

Needing some air, I step out onto the square patio. It's basically the fire escape and the size of a small coffee table, but still. It's mine.

The sounds of the city surround me, distant honking, tires shrieking against the pavement, voices blending and filling the night air with a distant murmur. It's the sound of home.

But when I look up, I can't see the stars.

Chapter Twenty-Four

I WAS ONCE TROUBLED by the many paths that lay before me so I decided to be admirable at everything.

–Cyrano de Bergerac

"Night, Beast."

Lucas passes me on the way to his car, and I throw him a two-fingered wave, waiting until his door is closed before shoving the key in my ignition. But before I put the truck in gear, I check my phone.

I miss you.

It's two a.m., way too late to write back. Or too early. Four a.m. in New York. My fingers hover over the keyboard. But then I toss the phone down on the empty seat and get moving.

Driving home from work isn't the same without Fred next to me. I glance over at her side of the cab.

Nothing is the same.

School is starting next month, and I've been trying to

distract myself until then by working as many hours as possible. When classes start, I'll still work part-time, helping after school in the kitchen at Bodean's for a few hours each night. Anything to keep my mind from lingering on the woman with a boy's name, the heart of an angel, and a tendency to ramble when she's nervous. It would take me a full twenty-four hours to reach her if I kept driving.

When I pass the tree where we used to park, I almost give in to the urge.

But when I reach the turnoff that stretches down to the ranch, I take it.

The next morning, Grace is in the kitchen, sitting on the counter with her laptop open next to her.

She jumps down when she sees me. "You want coffee?"

I nod and she practically flies to the machine to pour me a mug.

She's been doing this ever since Fred left.

"How was work?"

Fine, I sign.

"Are you hungry?" She smiles at me. "I can cook something for you. I'm really good at slapping together sandwiches and pouring milk into cereal."

I shake my head no.

Her smile droops and she pivots away, facing her laptop.

I grimace and rub a hand through my hair. I miss Fred. It's difficult to pretend otherwise. Grace has been doing her best to be positive and upbeat and make me feel better, but I know it's only because she's harboring guilt.

It's not Grace's fault. She's just a kid who already has enough to deal with. Staying is my choice. But part of me wishes I could leave. If I knew Grace would be okay, maybe I would go to New York.

I set down my coffee and walk over to her, leaning back against the counter so we're facing each other.

Are you coming with me today? I sign.

She nods. "Of course. I have an appointment later, too."

According to the doctors, my larynx is weak from disuse. The larynx itself is a muscle that houses the tissues and vocal cords used to create sound. I've got to strengthen those muscles in order to produce anything more than moans and shrieks. But first, I have to push through the swamping anxiety that threatens me every time I try.

After Fred left, I upped my sessions to three times a week. More than anything, I want to be able to talk to her. To *call* her.

Texting hasn't been completely awful. Some of the pictures Fred has sent me, along with the more explicit messages, are exhilarating, and yet they make the hole in my heart that much bigger. She also texts photos of land-marks, excited to show me every part of her city whenever I can visit, but I just want to spend that time with her in bed, exploring the parts of her body in the other photos she's sent.

I have to delete everything so Grace doesn't come across them while snooping on my phone. She doesn't do it to be cruel or anything, it's just part of her—tech is something that gives her a measure of control when the rest of the world feels like it's spinning out of it.

Even with the therapy, pushing anything through my throat continues to be difficult. It would be laughable if it weren't so pathetic. But difficult doesn't mean impossible. It's getting better—especially since meeting Fred—but loving her isn't a cure-all. There is no magic button. Every day, it will get a little bit better as long as I roll with the inevitable setbacks.

Setbacks like Fred's absence. Since she left, everything has been harder. Touching her helped. Taking care of her helped. Her taking care of me helped. Being understood, accepted without judgment. Not once did she make me feel less than, even when she knew everything.

The rest of my family helps, too, but it's not the same.

I'm going to get chores done before we leave, I sign to Grace and she nods.

"Beast," she calls before I can make it through the door.

I stop and face her.

Her mouth is a thin, colorless slash in her normally expressive face. "You're not happy."

I'm fine.

She sighs. "Make sure you close the coop door if you're checking on the eggs. Kylo Hen's been more ornery than usual."

~

Two weeks later, things are better and things are worse. I spoke a word in therapy. One clear, careful word, with proper enunciation and everything.

I've video messaged with Fred three times, which is wonderful and weird all at once. She's been practicing her ASL and we spoke using a combination of hands and texting, but at least we could also see each other. Her beautiful smile filling the screen is a double-edged sword of pleasure and pain.

The next morning I'm cooking breakfast for Jude and Reese. Jude levels me with a penetrating look. "Not sleeping?"

I shrug. I've been having problems falling asleep and staying asleep. It's something that used to be an issue, years ago. It had gotten better, but now . . .

"You smiled more when she was here."

I cut him a sharp glance.

"No reason to get cranky, big fella, that wasn't judgment upon your current level of stoicism." He pats me on the shoulder. "You have options. No one is forcing you to stay, not even the teenage menace to society."

My jaw clenches and I scowl at him. He knows why I can't leave.

Jude lifts his hands in a gesture of innocence. "I'm just sayin', we would all understand if you had to follow your own path. We won't ever stop being your family. Where you live isn't important."

I wish it were that easy.

Later in the week, my therapist prescribes me an anti-anxiety medication to help with the ongoing cognitive behavioral therapy.

Part of me recoils at taking pills, not only because of the side effects, but because I should be strong enough to work through things without medication. Physically, I can take on anything. I'm not used to feeling weak. But I know that's pride speaking. If it will allow me to progress to the point where I can speak with Fred, I'll crawl through broken glass to make it happen.

And then one Sunday, everything changes.

Granny has allowed me to take over Sunday supper duties, a miracle in and of itself.

She and Grace are target shooting in the backyard and I'm braising short ribs on the BBQ when Grace comes pounding up the porch, out of breath.

Are you okay? I sign, but she doesn't appear injured. She's smiling.

She shoves a thick white envelope in my hands. "This came for you today."

The return address is in New York.

I stare at her long enough and hard enough that she smacks me in the arm. "Open it."

As I tear open the envelope, the words on the paper blur before my eyes. It's an acceptance letter to the CIA, in New York. The one Fred told me about.

I blink to clear my vision, emotion gripping my throat, but this time it's not because of anxiety or apprehension.

My gaze flies back to Grace and holds.

She bites her lip. "I've been selfish. I can't hold you back from what you want. I love you. I care about what you want more than what I want. And you will be happier wherever she is." She swallows and then talks in a rush of words. "So I might have sort of hacked into your computer and stolen your résumé and sent it in. If you love me, you'll go. Because nothing is more important than your happiness. You are always looking out for everyone else, and it's time that someone looked after you."

I put my hands up to sign, but she stops me with a shake of her head.

"And it might be possible that the time you applied to that other culinary school in Dallas, maybe I made sure you wouldn't get in. But that was wrong, and now I'm trying to make it right. Besides," she continues, "if you had gotten in to the other place, then you never would have met Fred, so really I did you a favor."

Okay, even I can admit that's stretching. But still.

"It's my turn to sacrifice something for you," Grace says. "Just like you did when we lived with *he who shall not be named*."

I smile. Fred made Grace watch all of the Harry Potter movies over Christmas break. And then a week later, during a fit when Grace threw her laundry at Fred, Fred danced around yelling, "Dobby is free!" and Grace laughed so hard she cried.

I blink through a film of tears. Shake my head. How can this be real?

I sign, *How can I leave you behind? And I still can't talk.*

"Don't argue with me. A lot of people don't talk. And you're learning. You will talk. I know it. There's no reason you can't continue your voice therapy in New York. And maybe," she bites her lip and her head droops, "maybe I need to learn how to be on my own, too. But I'm not really on my own. We will always have each other no matter where you live. Jude and Granny and the rest of them won't let me be lonely. And I'll visit you. Please, Beast, follow your happy."

I yank her to me, hugging her tiny frame. When she was born, she almost fit in my hand, she was so tiny.

She pulls back first. "I had to pull some strings to make sure you could start when the next term begins in a month. And Granny wants another party before you leave, so it's going to get busy. Are you going to call Fred?"

My grin is so wide it hurts my cheeks.

Fred was the hero in her story, and now it's time for the rest of us to follow suit.

Chapter Twenty-Five

ALL THOSE LETTERS, they were you . . .

All those beautiful powerful words, they were you! . . .
The voice from the shadows, that was you . . .
You always loved me!
–Cyrano de Bergerac

"Do you want to come over later? We can watch a movie or something. I'll even let you feed me cupcakes."

Scarlett laughs, the sound tinny from my phone's speaker. "I would love to stuff your face with cake and frosting, I've got some new flavor ideas for the truck and I could use some advice, but Guy has something planned for us tonight."

"Oh." I sidestep a questionable puddle on the sidewalk. It hasn't rained in weeks. That's either booze or urine. "Maybe tomorrow? Or Sunday? I could use a distraction."

"You're not hanging out with your new friends tonight? I thought maybe you had plans."

"Nah, they're cool and all, but I didn't feel like being social."

I have hung out with my coworkers periodically over the past few weeks. I've gone for drinks, out for dinner, I even went to a movie with a fellow new hire. I'm practically a social butterfly. It's helped ease the incessant longing pushing at my heart, despite the excitement and gratification with my job.

I haven't talked to Beast as much lately. We've both been busy. And I can't help but wonder, is he slipping away? Will our calls and texts get more and more infrequent and eventually cease entirely?

"You don't want to be social, but you wanted me to come over?" Scarlett asks.

"With you I can be bleak and miserable. With my coworkers, I have to put on a face like I'm happy and normal."

She pauses. "Aren't you, though? Happy?"

I stop at a crosswalk, waiting for the light to change. "I mean. I am in some sense. I'm ecstatic about my job and apartment. But . . . I know, I can't base my entire happiness on someone else, and I'm not, but I miss him, Scarlett." I can't stop the thickness from entering my voice.

"I know, Fred. Why don't you go home, take a bath in that awesome claw-foot tub, order takeout, and call Beast? I bet you'll feel better."

I swallow. "You're right."

"And call me in the morning, okay?" There's something off in her tone, like she's distracted, but it's probably just Guy or one of the kids. I don't want to push her on it, and I've reached my building anyway. We hang up and I get out my keys for the front entryway.

The elevator has a *Do Not Use* sign so I trudge up the stairs. I guess it's a good thing. This is the only exercise I get. I exit the stairwell onto my floor and halt.

Down the hall, a large figure sits in the hall, head tipped back against my door, eyes shut.

Oh my Chuck.

"Beast?" The word, only a whisper, may as well be a gunshot.

He jerks up. Our eyes meet.

"Am I hallucinating?"

He smiles at me, shaking his head no. He lumbers to his feet, and I'm already running.

Heart pounding, I leap into him in a graceless move that should send us both sprawling to the floor. But he would never let me fall. He catches me, holding me up against him while I rain kisses all over his face.

I hold his face between my hands, tracing his features with my eyes. He's thinner. Grey smudges line his eyes, and there is enough stubble under my fingers to indicate he hasn't shaved since at least yesterday morning. "You're here. You're really here. I've imagined you here, but I can't believe this is real."

Then we're kissing again. I lift my legs to wrap them around his waist and he grasps my ass in his giant palms.

He leans back against my door, his mouth devouring mine like I'm a succulent dessert and he hasn't eaten in months. I start unbuttoning his shirt and then my neighbor's door opens and a whistle jars us out of our kissing trance.

Flushing, I unwrap myself from Beast but his hands don't leave me, touching my back, my shoulder even as I unlock my door and he picks up his bag from where it was sitting on the floor.

"Hey, I was enjoying the show!" my neighbor yells.

"Good night, Dave."

"I think yours is gonna be better than mine," he calls out as I shut the door.

We get inside the apartment and I lock the door. He drops his bag on the floor and then we're kissing again.

This time, it's not a consuming scorch of lips, but a tender expression of intent. Soft and sweet, full of heated emotion.

We pull apart, and I grasp his hand and lead him into the bedroom. It's not yet dark outside, though the sun has disappeared behind the buildings, casting the sky with an orange glow that seeps through the curtainless windows.

No words are needed as we undress each other, the only sounds the whisper of our clothing as it hits the floor.

He runs his knuckles over me, from my breastbone to my navel and back up. Tracing delicate patterns over my skin in effortless seduction. Then we're falling into bed.

He shifts over me, arms braced on either side of my head, the blunt head of him pressing against my sensitive entrance. His mouth sips at mine as he pushes inside, hard and insistent.

I grip at his lower back, pressing at him, rocking my hips to drive him deeper, but he's inexorable, the power of him a leashed force entering me barely an inch at a time. Finally, he pulls back from the kiss, our eyes locking, and he plunges the final inch. We shudder together, holding on to the moment. My hands glide up his body to close around his nape.

His gaze is raw, possessive, full of a primal heat that echoes inside me.

And then he moves. Our bodies rock in unison, a slow and tender dance. He lifts one hand to brush against my skin, cupping my breast, drawing circles around the sensitive peaks.

I lift my legs and lock around him, clasping him, guiding his movements into the perfect angle to thrust right *there.* Minutes later, pleasure ripples through me without warning, a wave that takes Beast out with me, and we're both groaning in the aftermath of release.

Sometime later, actual time has ceased to have meaning, but the room is dark and we're lying in bed, facing each other with my leg up over his waist.

"Are you hungry?" I ask, tracing the line of his shoulder with a finger.

He shakes his head. Then he reaches out and runs his thumb over my lips, his eyes following the movement before he meets my eyes.

"I love you." His voice is deep and soft, comforting like hot chocolate, the words hoarse.

I can't move. I can't think. I can only stare at him in awestruck wonder, my heart pounding.

"Beast," I manage to get out between frantic breaths. I push up to sitting and stare down at him. "You *talked.*"

His eyes widen in feigned shock. "I did?"

Stunned by both his words and the fact that he can make jokes at a time like this, I burst into tears.

He pulls me into his chest.

"You talked," I blubber all over him. "You told me you loved me. You're here. It's all so overwhelming I'm not sure I can take it."

His chest moves under my cheek, and I pull back to watch, holding my breath while he takes a couple long seconds to force out words again. "It's . . . hard."

The words aren't quite as confident as his profession of love. This time, his voice is forced, a little ragged with effort.

"It's okay." I hold his dear face, rubbing a thumb over the scruff on his jaw, meeting his eyes. "You don't have to. I don't care if you never talk again. You're perfect just as you are."

He smiles and nods. *I know*, he mouths.

"Maybe I should mention that I love you, too." I'm smiling so hard, my cheeks hurt.

His returning grin is blinding, the dimple in his cheek winking at me.

I sigh, completely infatuated with everything about him. If I were a cartoon, those little heart eyes would be popping out of my face right now.

"Oh." A thought occurs to me. "What if 'I love you' was all you could say? You could be like the romantic version of Groot." I widen my eyes, a little excited at the prospect. Beast is as probably as big as adult-sized Groot.

He pulls me down, kissing me even as his shoulders shake with laughter under my hands, his mouth curved up, smiling against my lips.

"Wait." I sit up before we can get sucked back into Sexy Land. "You might wanna grab your phone because I have a lot of questions. How long are you staying? Why didn't you tell me you were coming? When did you start talking?"

I slide off him and he rolls away, grabbing his phone from his pants on the floor while I continue my barrage of questions and rambling nonsense.

"We have to go to Dinosaur Bar-B-Que while you're in town. It's in Harlem, not quite like Granny does it, and well, maybe you could do it better but . . ."

He gets back in bed, holding up his phone.

I blink at the words on the screen, not registering it at first, like his phone is somehow converting the words to Dothraki.

I'm not going back to Blue Falls.

I read it twice. Meet his eyes. He nods. I read it a third time. And then a fourth. And I burst into tears all over again.

Minutes later, after I've pulled my shit together, he gives me the rest of the story. With his phone this time. He's met max capacity for speaking. He tells me about Grace applying to CIA for him, her admission that she interfered with his prior application, but now he's starting in less than a month. He even has a place to stay, since the school helped him find housing nearby.

"I wish you could live here with me." I run a hand down his stomach, watching his muscles flex and respond to my touch.

We both need to stand on our own, I think. For now.

"You're so wise for one so young."

I'll be a train ride away.

"Which is so much better than a plane ride and hours of driving."

We stay up half the night catching up on everything. We've been communicating since I left, but not as much recently—since, apparently, he was planning a cross-country move. We touch and talk. I tell him stories about my coworkers, he tells me stories from Blue Falls and what I've missed since I left. There are sexy times in between when we need a break from the talking and the touching and caressing brings us to the point of no return.

It's early in the morning, nearly sunrise, when I show him my "patio" so we can look up at the stars.

"I see one!" I point at one glimmering light in the sky. "Oh wait. That's a plane." I squint. "Maybe a drone?" I grin up at Beast. "Not quite like home, huh?"

His arms wrap around me and his voice is in my ear, hushed and raspy, but pure. "You are home."

Epilogue

"ONE THING I've learned is no one sticks by you like your friends. Especially here."

–Overheard at Comic-Con

Five months later . . .

"I want to do the polar bear plunge." Grace bounces around us on her toes, feet thudding against the wooden planks beneath our feet. Her cheeks are pink from the wind, blonde hair smothered under a bright pink beanie Fred bought her this morning.

"You want to jump in that freezing cold water?" Fred asks.

"Sure."

"The plunge is on the first." Fred's hand squeezes mine, the motion intimate even through our gloves. "And you're leaving tomorrow."

"Have you ever done it?" Grace asks, tone challenging.

"Uh, no, I avoid frostbite."

Grace rolls her eyes and skips ahead of us on the nearly empty boardwalk. "Maybe it will snow!" she calls over her shoulder.

"I wish it would," Fred tells me. "Then she could see her first snow and maybe her flight would get cancelled and she could stay a couple more days."

I squint up into the bright sunshine. It's cold, the breeze biting, but there are no clouds in sight. To our left, the Atlantic Ocean crashes onto an expanse of sand.

Grace has never seen the snow. We hoped she'd get her chance during this first trip to the city, but so far it's been nothing but sun. Cold, but no weather. She arrived a day after Christmas, and we had our own little holiday celebration. Snow aside, we've packed in as much as we could into the three-day visit, and now we've only got one more night.

"We should get some blintzes from Gourmanoff while we're here," Fred says.

What about dinner? I sign.

Fred lifts her brows at me with a grimace. "You really want to eat my mom's food?"

I grin and lean down to kiss the corner of her frowning mouth, turning the grimace into a smile. "She might surprise you." Talking is easier than it was six months ago. But not effortless.

"You're an optimist. And braver than I will ever be. I guess we should head back to the B train anyway if we're going to get to Park Slope on time."

She calls out for Grace, who is hanging on to a railing up ahead, looking out at the beach and water. She skips back and we walk together to the subway, Grace and Fred chatting about various tricks to make it look like you're eating when you're really just pushing your food around your plate.

The train ride is about forty minutes, Grace sitting between us, chattering the whole way about the New York Hall of Science—a science and technology museum in Queens we took her to yesterday.

Fred's mother, who insists I call her Helen, greets us in the entry of the brownstone.

"Let me take your coats." She hangs all of our outerwear on an antique coat rack in the corner and gives us all hugs in turn, gripping me tight and wrapping me in her lemony-basil scent. Crisp and clean and homey, like a mother should smell.

"Thank you for having us for dinner," Grace says meekly.

Fred and I exchange a glance. Grace is not herself around Fred's parents—not in a bad way, just in a non-Grace way. She's extra polite and doesn't talk much, like she's suddenly some foreign, shy creature and not the menace we know and love.

"Oh, honey, I'm the one who is happy you could make it. Come into the kitchen. I found something for you at the store." She takes Grace's arm and leads her away, hollering down the hall. "Larry, the kids are all here."

Indistinct muttering emerges from the depths of the house.

"Another present?" Fred calls after her Mom. "Where's my present?"

Helen and Larry bought Grace the coat and gloves she's been wearing as a Christmas present, knowing she wouldn't have anything like it and figuring she could keep it at Fred's for when she visits in the winter. I'm pretty sure Helen coordinated the surprise with Granny. They dropped the elegantly wrapped package off at Fred's apartment when Grace first arrived. Grace was so shocked by the gesture she didn't speak for five full minutes.

I'm not sure Grace knows how to react to the couple, not used to people being so open and affectionate. They welcomed both of us into the family without question. It's like being on a TV show or something.

Fred gives my arm a squeeze. "I'll make sure Grace isn't a pod person, intent on infecting Mom. You go and check on Dad. He probably needs to be 'encouraged' "—she makes air quotes with her fingers—"to come eat whatever questionable casserole we're having tonight."

"I'm not threatening your dad," I whisper.

"I never said anything about threats. Just make it happen."

I knock on the open office door before entering, and Fred's dad is up and out of his chair, clapping me on the back.

"Beast. Come on in, son, I want your opinion." He guides me over to the corner. "Helen bought me this stool for my office. What do you think?"

He points out the spindly piece of furniture—if it

could be called that. It's a bright purple cushion, set upon twisty thin black legs.

Instead of giving my opinion, I ask, "What is it for?"

Larry shrugs. "To torture me? Why don't you sit on it so we can test it out?" His eyes are gleaming.

You want me to break it, I sign.

"I didn't say that." He rubs his chin. "Maybe I want to test its strength."

I shake my head, but I'm smiling. *I can't do that. It might hurt Helen's feelings.*

Fred's parents were beyond excited to learn ASL. Like it was no big deal. And like I was doing them a favor, prompting them to gain some new knowledge. They've decided to learn British Sign Language next just for kicks.

He nods, rubbing his chin. "Maybe I can convince you after dinner. That will be the torture portion of the evening. Come on, time to face the music." We head into the dining room.

Fred and Grace are already at the table, Helen in the kitchen.

"I tried something new this week," Helen calls out. "It's about ready."

"Ready for imminent death," Fred mutters.

Grace presses her lips together, trying not to laugh.

I pull out my seat at the table next to Grace and across from Fred.

"Look what Helen gave me." Grace holds up a little snow globe and shakes it. It's got the New York skyline in the center, glittery flakes tumbling around. "Since I missed the snow this time."

Did you tell them thank you? I sign.

She releases a beleaguered sigh. "Of course." She places it gently beside her plate.

"Here we are." Helen brings out a casserole dish and lays it on a trivet in the center of the table. "Everyone, dig in. Who wants a drink?" She goes back into the kitchen to grab a soda for Grace and some water for the rest of us.

Fred and her dad exchange a glance. "You first," she says.

I smile and pick up the serving spoon, putting a heaping portion onto my plate.

"Are you sure that's a good idea?" Fred stage-whispers.

"I heard that." Helen comes back into the room with the drinks and sits at the head of the table, opposite Larry.

Everyone dishes food onto their plates.

Helen asks Grace about when school is starting while Larry talks to Fred about how engineers are designing toilets to analyze excrement for pre-diagnosing health issues.

"No poop talk at the table," Helen tells him.

I wait patiently for Fred to take a bite of her food and when she does, I'm not disappointed.

She chews for a second and then her brows hit her hairline. "Mom, what is this? This is actually . . ." Her expression is mystified, staring down at the dish like it's sprouted wings. "Good." She takes another bite. "This is good."

"Eggplant parmesan baked with homemade vegan mozzarella. I might have had some tips from Beast."

Fred's mouth pops open. "You listened to him? You never listen to me!" Her eyes flick to mine. "You gave her cooking advice?"

I sign, *I did it for you.*

Larry puts a hand on my arm. "It's better to remain silent when they get like this."

Grace is giggling so hard, she leans into me, shoulders shaking.

Fred is half laughing, half arguing with Helen, and Larry leans toward me, elbow on the table, sending my fork clattering to the floor.

The table is chaos, but joy is a squeeze in my chest. Happiness is the laughter of the people I love most. Happiness is chasing after my dreams. Happiness is . . . her.

Across the table, my eyes lock with Fred's and her smile lights up the entire room, brighter than any star.

About the Author

Go here to sign up for the newsletter! www.
authormaryframe.com

Mary Frame is a full-time mother and wife with a full-time job. She has no idea how she manages to write novels except that it helps being a dedicated introvert. She doesn't enjoy writing about herself in third person, but she does enjoy reading, writing, dancing, and damaging the eardrums of her coworkers when she randomly decides to sing to them. She lives in Reno, Nevada, with her husband, two children, and a border collie named Stella.

She LOVES hearing from readers and will not only respond but likely begin stalking them while tossing out hearts and flowers and rainbows! If that doesn't creep you out, email her at: maryframeauthor@gmail.com
Follow her on Twitter: @marewulf
Like her Facebook author page: www.
facebook.com/AuthorMaryFrame

Imperfect Series reading order:
Book One: Imperfect Chemistry
Book Two: Imperfectly Criminal

Book Three: Practically Imperfect
Book Four: Picture Imperfect
Book Five: Imperfect Strangers
Book Six: Imperfectly Delicious

The Dorky Duet (Plus a companion novel!)
Rirdorkulous
Geektastic
Nerdelicious

The Extraordinary Series
Anything But Extraordinary
A Life Less Extraordinary
Extraordinary World

Coming June 2021, a brand new rom com!
Time of My Life